NATIONAL BEST SELLING AUTHOR
YAHRAH ST JOHN

Unchained
Hearts

Chapter 1

"L ONDON, WHEN ARE YOU COMING back to Dallas for a visit? We miss you," Bree Hart said from the other end of the phone line on a Saturday evening in early April.

As London Hart sat on the sofa of her cozy three-bedroom cottage home in Mid-City New Orleans, eating a family-sized bag of potato chips, she snorted at her half-sister Bree. Despite London's divorce and the fact that her restaurant near the French Quarter was in the red, she was in no mood to go back to her hometown. Why should she be?

When London was ten, her mother, Loretta Watson, had picked up and moved the two of them from Dallas to New Orleans, where Loretta's parents lived. Loretta didn't hang around for long, but London had lived here ever since. So she'd never had a chance to feel like part of her father's side of the family, the Harts, who were based in Dallas. And that was just fine with her. Her grandparents Jeremiah and Grace Watson and her aunt Ella James and Ella's husband, Henry, had welcomed her with open arms and London had never looked back.

"I'm sorry. I don't know when that will be," London finally replied to Bree. Although they shared the same father, London and Bree couldn't be more different. London was feminine and liked all things delicate. Bree, on the other hand, was a rough and tumble tomboy and always wanted to be seen as one of the fellas.

In London's opinion, there were just some things that were better left off to men, and she wasn't afraid to say it. At nearly six feet tall, with a curvaceous, whopping size-eighteen figure, London was a lot of woman and she knew it. It would take a special man to realize that. And it would never be her ex-husband Shawn—that Negro wouldn't know a good woman if she slapped him in the face. How else to explain why he'd left London—who treated him good with sex on the regular and a home-cooked meal on the table every night—for a skinny-ass heifer named Eva.

"But you promised after Caleb's wedding that you would make more of an effort for us to get closer," Bree said, interrupting London's thoughts.

Did I say that? London wondered. Perhaps she really *had* acquiesced after Bree and their younger sister, Jada, had ganged up on her after their cousin Caleb Hart's wedding last year. She didn't like all the family drama, and that's exactly what happened every time the Hart clan got together: drama.

"And I will. Just not now," London replied. "It's been hard since the divorce. It's only been a year."

"Which is exactly why you need family at a time like this. Jada and I should come down."

London shook her head. "That's not necessary, Bree. Stay in Dallas, alright? It's not like I don't have family here. Don't worry about me, I've got this." And just as quickly as she could, London ended the call before Bree could keep ragging on her.

London glanced down at the time. *Crap!* She was supposed to meet her friend Violet Griffin for drinks at the Wishing Well and she was late. Jumping up, London headed for her bedroom in search of something to wear. She wasn't keen on Violet's hunt for the perfect man

2

tonight. She was sour on the opposite sex after Shawn, but she'd agreed to attend this dating event with Violet.

London flipped through the hangers in her closet until she came across a figure-flattering black jumpsuit. Add a large gold belt, dangling earrings, and high-heeled sandals, and she was ready for the evening.

It didn't take long for her to curl her chestnut hair until the curls framed her face, slick on a bit of a makeup, and be out the door in twenty minutes, speed walking to her Jeep.

She made it to the Wishing Well in fifteen minutes flat. The parking lot was already full with partygoers. Reaching for her small clutch, London exited the Jeep. As she headed for the door, she noticed several women ahead of her. They were dressed in slinky dresses that showed off their petite figures.

London looked down at her jumpsuit. By comparison, the other women made her look dumpy and frumpy. *Maybe I should turn around?* She was thinking this just when Violet came rushing toward her.

"London, there you are," her best friend said as she approached. "I thought you'd never get here."

At five foot two, Violet was a petite knockout. Side by side, London towered over Violet, casting a long shadow. But what Violet lacked in stature she more than made up for in confidence. She had thick, long black hair that cascaded down her back, and well, London would kill for Violet's figure. Violet had the kind of body that men called stacked—in all the right places. London could never understand why Violet was single when she made such an attractive package. Tonight was no different. Along with stiletto heels, she wore a fiery-red top with the shoulders cut out and skintight black leggings that had to have been sprayed on.

Violet slid her arm through London's and led her toward the front door. She breezed past the host manning the line with a quick "She's with me," before rushing London inside. The event was in full swing. Swarms of beautifully dressed people drinking beer, wine, or fruity cocktails filled the place.

"What do you want?" Violet asked as she squeezed her small fanny through the crowd while London had to go around people. Not only was London not the average size of most women in the room, she was a full head taller than them too. She definitely stuck out.

"I'll have an apple martini," London said, turning her back to the bar as she surveyed the crowd.

In her opinion, the place was filled with the usual suspects. There was the playboy who had a crowd of women surrounding him as he regaled them with some tall tell. There was one man, however, who caught her interest.

Why? Because he sat off from the crowd and was focused more on his drink than the pretty people around him and he wasn't dressed for the occasion. London could see he was quite attractive in a rugged sort of way. His hair was clipped short. He had bushy eyebrows and a groomed goatee surrounded by delicious full lips. His T-shirt showed off his broad shoulders and bulging biceps. Add his snug jeans, and she was sure he had to be holding a spectacular package. London liked a man's man and this man looked like he was definitely the sort. She licked her lips.

As if the man sensed he was being watched, he looked up and caught London's eye. She immediately looked away, embarrassed at having been caught staring.

Just then, Violet handed her a drink from her side. "Thanks," London said, then took a quick gulp.

"Easy, tiger," Violet said. "What's got you so jittery?"

"Nothing." London shrugged, but she could sense that now she was the one being watched. She could feel the stranger's eyes on her, checking her out. She took another sip of her drink.

"So, have you seen any prospects?" London asked, quickly changing the subject.

Violet shook her head. "No, not really. And I was so hopeful. It's hard being single."

"Don't remind me," London said. Since divorcing a year ago, she hadn't realized just how hard the single life would be. She'd been with Shawn for seven years, five of them married. So she hadn't been on the market in a long time. Now that she was, London missed the safety and security of being in a relationship. Dating in this new millennia was damn hard. The rules had all been thrown out. It was now perfectly acceptable to ask a man out or get his phone number. Back in the day, London would never have dreamed of being so forward.

"I was hoping that I could meet someone the normal way instead of online," Violet said, "but no such luck. I'm no competition for some of these women out here. These hoochies will *do anything or anyone.*"

"I hear you," London said as she tried to casually glance behind her. This time, however, she caught the stranger's eye and he boldly stared back at her. Neither one of them turned away until Violet snapped her fingers in front of London's face.

"Hello? What's got your attention?" Her eyes followed London's and found the source of her distraction. "Oh, he's yummy."

"Violet!"

"What?" Violet shrugged. "Don't tell me you weren't thinking the same thing."

London's cheeks burned at being called out, but Violet was right—the stranger was masculinity on a pair of two strong legs. Yet there was also an aura of mystery and danger surrounding him. *What is this stranger's story?* London wondered.

Chase Tanner turned away from the voluptuous beauty

that had caught his eye a moment ago and turned his attention back to the bottom of his tumbler of Scotch. Given the day he'd had, not even a beautiful woman would lighten his mood.

He'd hoped coming to New Orleans would be a fresh start for him after the demise of his ten-year marriage to Bianca. Finding her in bed with Owen, his sergeant and best friend, after returning from his deployment in Afghanistan, had just about killed him. Never in a million years had he imagined that his closest confidant would betray him with his wife. His wife!

Deep down, Chase blamed himself. Had he honestly expected loyalty and commitment to their marriage when he'd voluntarily signed up for his sixth deployment and been gone for a year and a half? But they'd made vows and his decision hadn't given her a license to cheat. He'd immediately divorced the lying, cheating slut but not before he kicked the living daylights out of Owen. Luckily, he'd already put in his retirement papers, and after a serious reprimand, they'd given him his freedom after twenty years in the service.

He'd thought about staying in Waco, Texas, his hometown, but after a less than satisfactory experience with Veterans Affairs looking for employment, he'd taken a hike. He'd stayed in Waco long enough to get his affairs in order before deciding it was time for a change of scenery. He'd picked New Orleans because his best friend, Mason Dillard, an Army veteran, lived there and worked for a construction company. He'd thought Mason might be able to help him land a job.

In addition to his friendship with Mason, one of the things Chase had going for him was his physique. He was in tip-top condition after endless five-mile runs every morning and because of those boring days in the deserts of Afghanistan and Iraq when he'd had nothing better to do but to eat, sleep, and work out. It was Mason and his physique that helped him finally earn a paycheck. Now, he worked for the same construction company that employed Mason.

Problem was some of the construction crew had a problem with him. Chase figured it had something to do with the fact that rather than keep him as one of the day laborers, soon after starting he'd been promoted to superintendent of the in-house crew and subcontractors. Chase was a born leader. He wasn't used to sitting in the backseat. He'd been prepared to do just that, however, but the owner of the construction company had other ideas.

This afternoon, he'd nearly gotten into a shoving match when a few of the men had refused to do as he'd asked. Mason advised him to walk away and take a breather. Pissed off, Chase had gone home briefly and then come to the bar to blow off some steam and relax. Except when he got here, he'd learned some dating website had booked the place. The barkeep had let him in on the sly since he'd become a frequent visitor.

Chase planned on keeping to himself. *Or should I?* Perhaps a night with one of these willing females might do the trick to lift him out of his funk. He'd had a healthy amount of hookups post-divorce. Because he'd been with only one woman for a decade, he had a lot of catching up to do. Of course, he'd had no idea what he was in for.

Women today were much more forward than he was used to. In the two hours he'd been here, four women had approached him and given him their number. Didn't they know that an alpha male like him appreciated the chase? He'd sent each of them packing with a frown. But the honey with the tumble of ringlets, breasts that were more than a handful, and an ass he wouldn't mind spanking intrigued him.

She wasn't chasing. In fact, she was being coy. She was going to make him work for it. And boy, would he work it all night long.

Rising from his barstool, Chase slid a ten toward the barkeep and headed toward the object of his desire. On his way, he was stopped by yet another forward female.

"Can I get you a refill?" the slender woman asked. By comparison to the voluptuous beauty he was headed for, this woman looked anorexic. Chase preferred a gal with some meat on her bones.

"No thank you," Chase murmured and scooted past her just as fast as he could.

When he arrived at the object of his desire, the buxom lady had her back to him, but her friend, a pretty black-haired woman, turned around to face him.

"Good evening," he said, flashing her a smile.

"Hi," she said, smiling back. "I'm Violet and this is my friend London." She nudged London with her shoulder.

Chase swallowed as the woman turned around to face him and he came in full contact with the chestnut beauty. From far away, he hadn't be able to tell the color of those ringlets, but now he could and he looked forward to running his fingers through them. But it was her eyes that captivated him. They were slanted and almond-shaped and he was immediately lost. From her youthful appearance, he surmised she was around thirty.

"And your name?" She spoke to him directly.

Chase blinked several times, trying to escape the trance her eyes held him in. "Chase Tanner." He offered her his hand.

She accepted and when he grasped her delicate hand in his, he realized just how silky soft her skin was compared to his rough hands. "Pleasure," she said, smiling warmly at him.

"Can I get you ladies a refill?" he asked, motioning his head to the nearly empty drink in her hand.

"You can absolutely get *her* one," Violet said. "I'm going to leave you two alone so you can get better acquainted."

She grasped her martini glass and he noticed she gave London a conspiratorial wink as she departed.

Chase used the opportunity to slide into the space Violet had vacated so he could be closer to London. "So, how about that drink?"

London flung her curls aside. "I suppose another couldn't hurt."

Chase spun around to face the bartender. "She'll have another one of..." His voice trailed off.

"An apple martini," she offered.

He pointed to her—"What she said"—and turned back around as he leaned his back against the bar. "So, why haven't I seen you here before?"

"Do you frequent the bar?"

He shrugged. "The crew and I come here sometimes after work."

London nodded. "Well, I don't have much time for socializing. My restaurant keeps me pretty busy. As you can probably tell, I eat well."

He frowned. "Don't do that. Why would you put yourself down?"

London downed the remainder of her martini before placing the empty glass on the bar. *Why did I just stick my foot in my mouth?* This good-looking man had purposely come over to talk to her and here she was putting herself down as usual. "Habit, I suppose." The bartender slid a new martini her way. "Thank you."

"You shouldn't make it one," Chase said. He scooted closer until their elbows touched. Then he allowed his eyes to roam across every inch of her, from her red-painted toes peeking out from her high-heeled sandals to the delectable curve of her hips to her ample breasts. "I, for one, like everything that I see. Matter of fact, if you'd allow me, I'd love to take you back to my place."

London blushed scarlet and seconds later she threw her martini right in his face.

Chase stumbled backward, wiping away the liquid with his hands. "What the hell was that?"

"Do you always proposition women in bars?"

Wide-eyed, Chase stared back at her in utter disbelief. "Yeah, I do and they don't seem to mind. They usually welcome it."

The bartender chuckled behind the bar and slid some cocktail napkins Chase's way, which he promptly used to wipe his face.

"Well, I, for one, don't. I'm not that kind of woman, Chase Tanner. I want to be respected, not looked at as some object for your pleasure. But if you're looking for that type, I'm sure there are plenty of women here that would love to share your bed. Take your pick." Spinning on her heel, London snatched her clutch off the bar and stalked toward the exit, but not before Violet reached her at the door.

"What the hell happened?" Violet asked, her eyes wide with amazement. "I thought everything was off to a good start."

London turned back to glare at Chase, who was watching her from the bar as he blotted his T-shirt with a napkin. "So much for first impressions," London said, snorting. "He actually had the nerve to ask me back to his place."

"And?" Violet inquired. "What would be so wrong with that? He looks like just the type to be able to blow your back out."

"Violet!"

"C'mon, London. Didn't you tell me it's been awhile since, you know, you've been with a man? Wouldn't it have been nice to be held, touched... desired? I know I could sure use it."

"Yeah, well, it would only last one night and what then? Tomorrow morning I'd be back to being alone. No thank you. I'm heading home."

"Wait, I'll come with you."

London shook her head fervently. "No, you stay here and have fun. I wouldn't be much company anyways. I'll call you later."

"Alright, wish me luck."

Seconds later, London was in her car and on her way home to get in her pajamas and watch *Good Times* on TV One.

This woman actually threw a drink in my face? Chase was shocked by London's ballsiness. He was used to women who knew the score, but London was clearly different. She wanted to be respected, valued and not just for her figure. He also believed that she'd wanted him to come over. When he'd been at the bar, she'd sent him clear signals that she'd wanted his attention. He'd seen desire in her eyes.

But perhaps he'd come on a little strong? Had he lost his game? He could have approached her with a bit more finesse instead of what he actually did do—go straight to the basics, telling her in no uncertain terms that he wanted to sex her six different ways from Sunday. *Damn! I royally messed that up.*

Chase leaned back against the bar and surveyed the crowd. None of these women remotely caught his interest like London had. She was not only beautiful and sexy as hell, but she also had morals and values. He appreciated that, which is why he wanted a second chance. Maybe next time he'd make a better impression. He glanced around the room and found her friend Violet chatting with a bunch of females. He would need her help if he wanted to find out the name of London's restaurant. The lady had definitely sparked his curiosity.

Chapter 2

THE NEXT DAY, LONDON WAS happy to be back to work at her restaurant, Shay's—it took its title from her middle name, Shay, because she thought it was catchy. She'd mastered cooking as if she'd been born to do it. Interactions with men she had not. London still couldn't believe the audacity of Chase Tanner at the bar. Had there been a sign on her forehead that said *EASY?* Clearly, there must have been. How else to explain the bold way Chase had come on to her?

London was still smarting over the episode when she opened Shay's at seven a.m. to start making Sunday brunch. Their brunch was one of their biggest moneymakers of the week. The community always came out in force to get some of her fried chicken, macaroni and cheese, and collard greens after church. In addition to the usual soul food fare, London also offered chicken and waffles, crepes, and Eggs Benedict.

London liked having a well-rounded menu, but more importantly she loved what she did. Cooking had come as naturally to her as running track had come to her tomboy sister, Bree. London had the brains to do other things— she'd started out on another track when she earned her marketing degree at Tulane. But once she'd started working in corporate America, she knew that particular nine-to-five grind just wasn't her thing and she longed for something more.

When she was younger, she'd loved being in the kitchen with her grandma and helping her cook Sunday dinner. It was the only time London felt a sense of normalcy. Her mama was always out in the streets or leaving London with her grandparents to chase some man. As a child, they'd moved from pillar to post as Loretta Watson searched for the elusive great love. She never found it. Instead, she found a multitude of losers.

Eventually, London's grandparents had asked Loretta for custody of London. London could remember her grandfather lobbying for her. "Let her come and live with us," he'd said. "We love having her here. Makes us feel young." But her mother had put up a fuss. "I can't leave my baby." Grandpa Jeremiah had put his foot down. "You've been doing that already, Loretta. You're gonna leave London here with us."

He'd stated it rather than asked and finally her mama had given in. Living with her grandparents had been exactly what London had needed. She finally had a loving, stable home. She never had to worry about whether they would forget to pick her up from school or leave food in the refrigerator or worry about how her mother's boyfriends looked at her maturing figure.

At the ripe old age of nine, London had begun getting breasts. And by ten, she wore a B-cup and had more curves than most girls her age. Boys started paying her more attention at school and so had her mother's boyfriends. It had been a welcome relief when Grandpa Jeremiah had taken her into their home.

And that's how her love affair with cooking had begun. It had been subtle at first. As she'd grown older, she'd watch her grandmother in the kitchen. Then she'd pitch in with baking cookies, brownies, and cupcakes for school. By the time she was thirteen, she was not only helping her grandma in the kitchen, but she was actually making dishes herself.

Slam.

The sound of the back door prompted London to return to the present just as one of her line cooks, Charlotte, came walking through it.

"Well, good morning," Charlotte said with surprise when she caught sight of London already in her chef's coat. "What are you doing here so early?"

"Couldn't sleep, so I thought I'd get up and get started prepping for brunch. I'm hoping we sell out the place like we did last week," London commented.

Business had been slow for the last few months, but she was hoping that the upcoming New Orleans Jazz & Heritage Festival would bring in some much needed tourists for her struggling restaurant. Most of her family, including her Grandma Grace, had tried to persuade her to sell it after the divorce, but London wasn't having it and had bought out Shawn's shares.

Opening the restaurant had been her dream and she wasn't willing to throw in the towel just yet. Luckily, her grandfather was still on her side and had encouraged her to fight for what she believed in. Her father, Duke, the owner of a flourishing Dallas-based oil company, had offered her a handout, but London didn't want or need his money. She'd grown up the majority of her life without a father. It was a little late for him to start playing Daddy.

"What do you need me to get started on?" Charlotte inquired, putting on her chef's coat.

"How about starting on the trinity for the gumbo?" London asked, pointing to the celery, onion, and green pepper trio that were the stars of any real gumbo.

"I'm on it."

They continued most of the morning chatting as they each completed their respective tasks. When it neared eleven a.m., London's second cook came in to relieve

London so she could run home for church. As was her habit, she went to church every Sunday morning with her grandparents as she'd done for the last twenty years.

Traffic was still light for that time of morning and London made it home in twenty minutes. She was showered, shaved, and shined thirty minutes later and in her Sunday finest attire. She was wearing a simple navy fit-and-flare dress with low-heeled sandals. At her height, if she wore heels she would tower over folks and she wasn't eager to be the talk of the church.

Grabbing her keys from the nearby hook by the door, London headed for church. She arrived at noon, just as the second service was taking place. The reverend was already at the pulpit leading the choir into the first song to start the service. She squeezed into the pew beside her grandparents.

"You're late," her grandmother admonished.

"Sorry, Grandma," London whispered. "Time got away from me at the restaurant."

"Which is why you should give it up now that that no-good husband of yours is gone."

"Grace, hush," Grandpa Jeremiah said and leaned across his wife to reach for London's hand. "London is doing what she thinks is best."

"Humph!" Her grandmother was less than pleased with his response.

London smiled as she shook her head. She was glad to see that nothing had changed.

After the service, London, her grandparents, her aunt Ella and Ella's husband, Henry, stood outside the church. "That was a good service, wasn't it?" Aunt Ella asked.

London nodded.

"I think it was more for the young congregation than anything," Uncle Henry added, "about being mindful of the sins of the flesh."

Her grandfather laughed. "Young folks aren't the only

ones," he commented. "I know a few grownups that could stand to heed the lesson." He eyed London and she read his mind.

He was thinking about Shawn and how he'd cheated on London. Because her faith was important to her, it had been a prerequisite that Shawn join her church and he'd acquiesced. Now, however, London doubted he'd heard a word that was said. He'd been so quick to break his wedding vows.

Looking back, London wondered if she ever should have slept with him to begin with. Maybe if she'd been more discerning and kept her legs closed as the reverend had always taught her, maybe she wouldn't have ended up alone and childless at the age of thirty-two.

"I'm going to head back to Shay's," London said, cutting into the conversation.

"Must you?" Grandma Grace asked.

"It's my *business*, Grandma."

"I know, but you could come over to Sunday dinner."

"No can do," London said, "but I'll see you soon." And before her grandmother could get another word in edgewise, London waved and made a beeline for her Jeep. Otherwise, if she didn't, it would be the same old song about London closing up Shay's.

London arrived at Shay's a short while later and was happily surprised to see a line forming outside the door. Her hostess Nina was already taking names for the waiting list. It was shaping up to be a good day. It was true about what they said: Good things come to those who wait.

Chase pulled down the mirror in his Ford F-150 to eye himself in the mirror. He'd just arrived at Shay's, but hadn't yet gone in. If he was honest with himself, he was a bit nervous. He'd never been turned down by a woman and he had to admit, it had rankled him. He was used to women chasing after him, not the other way around. But London had made it clear that she was a woman to be respected. He appreciated that.

The thought of actually having her in his bed was even more of a turn-on. Would she be just as feisty in bed as she was out of it? Of course, the road to his bed wouldn't be as easy a journey as it had been with the other women he'd encountered. If he was interested in getting intimate with London and cocooning his head between that deliciously large bosoms of hers, he was going to have to charm her.

He hadn't had to woo a woman, since, well, since never. His ex-wife, Bianca, hadn't been a woman interested in social graces and traditional values. If she wanted something, she went for it, which is probably why she'd wasted no time tossing him aside when he was gone and another man came into the picture.

Chase blinked several times. He had to forget Bianca. That phase of his life was over. He was on a new path with his sights set on a new woman.

Exiting the vehicle, Chase headed for the restaurant door, bypassing several waiting guests. When he entered the place, the hostess greeted him. "Welcome to Shay's."

"Thank you," Chase said, giving her his best grin. "So what's it going to take for me to get a seat in here?" He glanced around and noticed that each table was filled to capacity. The restaurant was small but cozy, with only about fifteen tables and one large high top.

The hostess glanced around. "As you can see, we're pretty booked."

"C'mon," Chase said. He leaned against the doorway, revealing crazy-strong biceps rippling out of his muscle shirt and muscular thighs straining against his tight jeans. "There has to be something you can do."

"Well..." The young girl blushed. "There is a large table top over there," she said, inclining her head. "If you don't mind sitting with some strangers, I could probably squeeze in a place setting."

Chase grinned broadly, revealing white teeth. "Excellent," he said. He reached across the space between them and touched her arm. "I knew you would help a brotha out." As he did so, out of the corner of his eye he noticed movement and saw the swing doors close.

Omigod! Omigod! He's out there, London thought. She was about to head out to greet her customers while she was still in her Sunday best clothes when she'd seen *him:* Chase Tanner, the sexy, but arrogant man from the bar. Was she upset with him because his pick-up technique had lacked finesse? Or was her negative response to him a defense mechanism because she didn't want him or anyone getting too close?

Since Shawn left her, London had steered clear of dating and sex. Although it had been a year, she was still uncomfortable with getting back into the dating scene; and to meet Chase on her first attempt was disconcerting to say the least. She wasn't equipped to deal with a man as ruggedly sexy as him.

And that's exactly what came off him in droves: SEX.

When she'd opened the door and saw him standing there in that fitted shirt and jeans, she'd freaked out and rushed back into the kitchen. London wasn't a novice in the sex department. She'd been with Shawn and a handful of other men before him, but she didn't consider herself experienced in the slightest as to what would please a man like Chase Tanner.

Why am I even thinking about this? London shook her head. She wouldn't get close enough to Chase to find out. It's why she'd come back to the kitchen. So much for greeting her guests; she would just have to stay here until he left.

Chase smiled as he sat back on his barstool, thanking the hostess for procuring an available seat for him at the open table top. The other couples at the table didn't mind the intrusion.

Before perusing the menu, Chase glanced at the swinging louvered doors to the kitchen. He was positive that he'd seen someone come through them only to immediately go back inside. *Was it London? Did she see me and run in the other direction?* There was only one way to find out. He would stay until she had no choice but to come out and talk to him.

Several menu items looked appetizing to him. Living the single life, he wasn't used to getting a lot of home-cooked meals these days, but anything was better than the ready-to-eat meals from his Army days. He smiled when he saw London's face on the back of the menu next to a short bio on how she'd started in the restaurant business.

When the waitress came to take his order, he settled on gumbo, shrimp etouffee, and a sweet tea.

She was about to walk away when he asked, "Hey, is the owner and head chef here today?"

"London?" the waitress asked. "Oh yes, she's in the kitchen. Would you like to meet her?"

So it *had* been her he'd seen running back to the kitchen. *I knew it!* "Um, yes, I would. As I'm sure all these fine folks here would as well," he said, inclining his head toward several of the other patrons sitting at the high top across and beside him.

"Oh yes," a woman beside him chimed in. "I want to tell her that the short ribs were off the chain."

"Of course," the waitress said. "She might be on the line, so it could be a few minutes, but I'll be sure and let her know that you'd like to meet her."

"Thank you," Chase said with a grin. If London was hiding from him, she wouldn't be able to much longer. He'd set up a nice trap for her with no way out.

"You what?" London snapped sharply at the waitress.

"I'm sorry, Miss London," the waitress said, bowing her head. "I know you always like to come out and mingle with the guests. I'm sorry if I misspoke."

London let out a long sigh. She shouldn't snap at the poor girl. It wasn't her fault London didn't want to see Chase Tanner again. The waitress had done her job as she'd been trained to. "You're fine," London replied. "I'm sorry for snapping. Tell them I'll be out soon."

"Soon" for London was nearly an hour later, after Chase's first course of her homemade gumbo and second course of shrimp etouffee had gone out.

Taking off her apron, London walked to her small office so she could check out her appearance. Closing the door so she could see the full-length mirror behind it, London smoothed her clothes and fluffed out her hair. Her lips were bare because she'd eaten off half her lip gloss in the kitchen. She snatched her purse off the hook and touched up her lips. Pinching her cheeks, she said, "This will have to do."

Several minutes later, she swung open the doors into the main restaurant. She felt Chase's eyes on her almost immediately. It was as if they were boring into her, but she refused to look his way. Instead, she started at the far side of the room, thanking guests for coming out, making sure they were enjoying their meal and accepting their compliments on the food.

By the time she made it to the high top, London felt like she was mentally prepared to face Chase. She was wrong.

As soon as he turned his head and those deeply set, dark-brown eyes zeroed in on her, London lost all speech. She stared blankly at him trying to think of something to say, but she was at a complete loss.

"London, right?" Chase offered her his hand. "Nice place you have here."

London swallowed. "Th-thank you. And your food?" She looked down at his empty plate. "I trust it was to your liking?"

He grinned unabashedly. "You can't tell?" he asked with a chuckle as he patted his flat stomach. "The meal was mighty fine indeed."

"Thank you."

"No, *thank you*," he said, grinning. "My compliments to the chef."

Several of the patrons beside him concurred, congratulating her on serving such a fine meal. London tried to focus on what they were saying, but she could see Chase out of the corner of her eye, sizing her up. Or should she say, undressing her with his eyes. There wasn't a curve he missed as he completed a thorough assessment of her before returning to her face.

"I'm so glad you all enjoyed it," London said, smiling at the table's occupants. "You're going to think you died and have gone to heaven when you try my famous sweet potato pie. Enjoy your evening." She gave them a quick wave and began to walk away, but Chase touched her arm. A tingle went straight through London and she let out a low moan. Chase smiled. Had he just heard her involuntarily respond?

"London, can we speak later when you're off work?"

London glanced down at her watch. It was a little after nine-thirty p.m. and the restaurant wouldn't close until eleven and then she'd have to clean up. "That's going to be awhile," she responded. "Sundays are my busiest night."

"I'll wait."

London stared at him in disbelief. "Chase, that's really not necessary. It's going to be at least two to three hours before I'm finished."

He smiled. "I like the way you say my name. Say it again."

London blushed scarlet. She wasn't trying to be coy or flirtatious, but he was definitely taking it there. "You're incorrigible!"

"I know. I'll see you in a bit." He motioned to the waitress. "Can I have a piece of sweet potato pie and a coffee?"

London couldn't believe it. Chase Tanner was determined to wait her out and was digging in his heels. "Fine," she muttered as she headed to the kitchen. "Fine."

Two hours later, Chase sat atop his F-150 as he waited for London to close up shop. He'd spent an extraordinary amount of time eating his dessert and getting a refill on his coffee until finally, at closing time, he'd had to leave. And so, he'd sat in his truck waiting for London to come out. He wasn't going to give her a chance to run away again, not when he so desperately wanted to spend time with her.

London emerged from Shay's slightly before midnight. At the sight of her, Chase stood up straight. He watched her lock the door and turn around to leave. The astonished look on her face told Chase she'd expected that he'd long since retired and gone home. She'd underestimated him.

"Chase—"

"Can I walk you to your car?"

London pointed down the nearly deserted street. "It's just at the end of the block." She started toward it without waiting for him.

"I don't mind." Chase fell into step beside her.

"Are you always this pushy with women," London asked, "or is it just me?"

Chase chuckled. "I wouldn't call it pushy. I would call it showing interest."

London stopped midstride and spun on her heel. "And

you're interested in me. Why? Is it the way I look?" She motioned down her body. "Been there, done that." She started walking again toward her car.

"So you think men just want you for your body?"

London snorted. "I'm not blind, Chase. I see the way you and other men look at me. I have a big ass and large breasts. You can't wait to hit that. Am I right?"

Chase lowered his head. He had the decency to be embarrassed because she was right. She had a banging body and she knew it. So he had to choose his words carefully. "I admit that I *am* attracted to you. I think that was obvious last night. But I would like to take you out if you're willing to give me a chance."

They reached her car and London stopped at the driver's door. "And why would I do that? You made it quite clear from the start what you want from me, Chase."

"I can't lie. I like what I see, but I won't know what's underneath the hood unless you allow me to take it for a spin." As soon as he said that, Chase knew his choice of words was poor.

"Exactly what I thought, Chase." London used her remote to unlock her door and swung open her car door. "Good night."

"Wait!" Before he could say another word, she'd already slammed her door shut and was cranking her engine. *Damn!* How had he managed to screw up his chance with this woman yet again? He wasn't used to striking out.

He watched in disbelief as she pulled her Jeep away from the curb, leaving him standing alone on the deserted street. Chase didn't know what he would have to do to prove to London Hart that he was on the up and up and wanted her for more than just her body.

But somehow, someway, he would figure it out.

Chapter 3

"HE SAID WHAT?" VIOLET ASKED when she and London met up midweek for happy hour at their favorite hangout.

"You heard me," London snapped. "Honestly, Violet. I really can't believe this man. Right when I was thinking perhaps I'd misjudged him, he goes and puts his foot in his mouth."

Violet laughed. "I'm with you on this one. He really didn't win you over. But I just thought he would."

London's brow furrowed. "What do you mean?"

"Uh nothing." Violet reached for a tortilla chip and dipped it in the spinach and artichoke dip. She reached for another, but London grabbed the tray and held it away from her.

"Oh no you don't," London said. "Explain what you meant by the comment 'you thought he would.' "

Violet let out a long exaggerated sigh. "Alright, I'll come clean, but only if you return the dip you're holding hostage."

London returned the platter to the table. "Spill."

"After you left the dating event Saturday, Chase came over to me and asked if he could have your number. I told him unequivocally no way, no how. I didn't know if he was a stalker or something."

"But?" London said. "I feel a 'but' coming on."

"But I did give him a hint and told him that you owned

Shay's and that he should look you up. I honestly wasn't sure if he was blowing smoke up my ass, but clearly he was for real about reaching out to you."

"He did a bang-up job," London said, rolling her eyes. "Every time I'm with that man he ends up insulting me."

"I don't think it's intentional," Violet replied, munching softly on a chip. "I mean, he did wait for you to get off work to speak with you privately."

"Only to tell me he needed to test drive me," London snorted. "The nerve."

"What's really got you so fired up about this man?" Violet asked with a raised brow. "If I didn't know any better, I would think you wanted him to prove you wrong and come correct."

London sat back in her chair. *Is Violet right? Is that the real reason I'm so bummed out?* It had been a long time since a man had shown genuine interest in her. Yet by the same token she wanted it to be about more than her body. For years, she'd been self-conscious thanks to the jeering looks men had sent her way. She was disappointed that Chase's interest in her was only a means to an end: getting her in his bed. If that's all she was interested in, she could have hooked up with a number of men over the past year, but that wasn't who she was.

"Is that so wrong?" London asked. "That I want more than a casual fling?"

"Of course not," Violet responded. "I just wanted you to be honest about how you feel about the situation."

"There is no 'situation,'" London replied, making air quotation marks. "I'm sure after being shot down a second time, Chase Tanner won't be coming back for more."

"Thanks for asking me to come today," Chase said to his friend Mason as they hammered studs into the drywall at a home in the town's Ninth Ward. At six foot five and weighing close to three hundred pounds, Mason was just as good with a hammer as Chase since they'd helped rebuild bridges and homes in Afghanistan. Now, however, on this early Saturday morning they were volunteering for Habitat for Humanity and helping to rebuild homes in a community that Hurricane Katrina had ravaged ten years ago. Although a lot of neighborhoods had been rebuilt over the years, there was still work to be done.

Chase was down for some manual labor because he had tension to work off. It had been nearly a week since London had given him the brushoff and he was still smarting over it. He'd never had to make an effort to get a woman in his bed. Bedding women had always come easy to him even before he was married. It had started when he'd sprouted several inches over the summer before sophomore year in high school and packed on fifteen pounds of muscle when he'd joined the wrestling team. After that, suddenly the girls and women started paying him notice and it had been that way ever since.

But London was making him throw out his rulebook.

"Chase, what's up with you?" Mason asked as he stopped hammering. "You seem a little distracted. Everything alright?"

Chase nodded. "Yeah, man. I just have an itch that needs scratching."

"Sounds like a serious problem." Mason chuckled, eyeing him suspiciously.

Chase snorted. "It's not that kind of itch. It's a female."

"Ah, of course. Who's got you twisted?" asked blue-eyed, sandy-brown-haired Mason. Though he was white, he'd served with Chase in an Army unit that was primarily African American. He had picked up his buddies' slang.

"I don't think you would know her. Name's London Hart."

"Nope, doesn't sound familiar. You've always had an easy time of it with the ladies," Mason replied. "When we were stationed in Germany, the women were falling all over you."

"Well, this one isn't. Matter of fact, she's given me the boot *twice*."

"Wow! That's unusual for you, partner. So why don't you just move on? There's plenty more fish in the sea."

Chase thought about what Mason said. And he was right. There were lots of other women out there, but none had piqued his interest like London Hart. Maybe it was because she was more discerning than most, which is why she appealed to him. The fact that she had integrity spoke volumes. "Nah, I want *her*."

And he intended to have her. He just had to figure out how.

"Why do you always have to be late, Violet?" London queried for the third time as Violet pulled them into a parking space near the Habitat for Humanity worksite.

"I'm sorry," Violet apologized again. "I told you I overslept. Some of us are not used to getting up at this ungodly hour."

London glanced down at her watch. It read seven a.m. They were reporting to the site nearly an hour after their scheduled start time. She hated that they were late but still wanted to make a contribution to her community. She was sporting some ripped denim jeans and an oversized Habitat for Humanity T-shirt over a tank along with some sneakers. She'd come dressed to work.

When they walked onto the job site, it was as London expected—the project was already in full swing. London rushed over to one of the volunteers wearing a similar T-shirt. "Where's the superintendent?"

"Over there," the young man said, pointing to a large surly looking dude.

"Thanks," London replied and turned to Violet, who was

fussing with her hair. "You might as well stop primping 'cause we're about to get all hot and sweaty."

"Whatever." Violet rolled her eyes but followed London as she headed toward Matt, the leader of the project.

Matt was less than pleased with their late arrival. He'd have to repeat himself about the on-site training/tutorials on tasks they were assigned. Nonetheless, he did and then he gave each of them a hardhat and told them where they were most needed. The slab had already been completed. Work had already begun on framing the home, and they would be assisting with the effort.

"I need you both to head over to Chase," Matt said, motioning toward the home, "and he'll help you get started."

London's breath hitched. "Excuse me? Did you say 'Chase'?"

"Yeah, he's heading up framing for the home. Go on now." He shooed them off and returned to the task he'd been working on before they'd interrupted them.

"Did you hear that?" London turned to Violet with a frown.

"I have two ears."

"Don't be cross. He said Chase is heading up framing. It has to be Chase Tanner. The name is not used often in these parts. What's he doing here? Is he following me or something?"

"How could he be following us, London? He was here first."

"I'm going to find out." London began stalking over toward the home. She glanced behind her and Violet was hot on her heels.

Though she'd last seen him nearly a week ago, as soon as she approached, London knew it was him—she hadn't been able to get his image out of her mind all week. His back was broad and tapered to a slim waist. Even through the confines of his T-shirt, she could see his rippling muscles underneath. She tapped his shoulder. "Chase."

Hearing his name, he spun around to face her. "London? What are you doing here?"

Heat exploded in her palm and streaked up her arm at merely touching him, but she recovered and said, "I could ask you the same thing."

"Well, like you, I'm here to help," Chase responded, then glanced down at his watch. "And unlike you, I was on time."

London instantly blushed at the rebuke because he was right. "That's beside the point," she replied haughtily. "How did you know I was going to be here?"

Instead of answering her question, he pushed past her toward a nearby table that held an assortment of tools. He selected two drills and a box of studs and came back toward her. "Here," he said, handing her and Violet a drill, "you'll need these." He also gave London the box of studs.

He began walking toward the side of the home. London followed behind him but had to trot to keep up with his long strides. "Hey, I asked you a question."

He turned around to face her. "And I'm choosing not to answer. We have work to do here, London. We have a home to finish. I don't have the time nor the inclination to address your insecurities."

He took the box of studs out of her hand and then proceeded to show her an example of how to complete the task. "When you're done, come get me and I'll show you what's next." Seconds later, he gave her back the box and he was gone.

"Did you see that?" London asked with her hands on her hips.

"Yeah, I did," Violet replied, grabbing a stud and following suit like the example Chase had just showed them. "He put you in your place. Clearly, he had no idea that you were going to be here. And like you, he wants to make a difference. So can we get started?"

London rolled her eyes. "Fine." But she couldn't help

staring after Chase's retreating figure and wondering what it was about the man that got under her skin.

Chase couldn't believe his luck as he watched London from the sidelines. The object of his desire was right here in front of him. He'd thought he'd never get another opportunity to win her over and now it had just landed in his lap. Some might say his approach just now wouldn't win him any brownie points, but Chase knew better.

She was somewhat awkward with the drill, but to him London was all graceful movements. Whenever she was around him, a strange, yet slow burn hit him in the gut. He'd never burned for any woman. Never wanted any woman as much as he wanted London. But she was a tigress. London wouldn't appreciate a weak man or one who kept coming around her like a puppy dog. She would respond to action—decisive action.

And just now, he'd given it to her.

He'd shown her he was no pushover. It was time Chase started leading their encounters, instead of reacting to them. It was time he showed her who was boss.

London and Violet, along with several other volunteers, completed one side of the framing they were assigned before Chase called them over into a huddle.

"Now that we've finished framing, it's time we start," Chase said.

London listened from the periphery of the group. She didn't want to get any closer to Chase than she needed to. She was much more attracted to him than she cared to admit to herself or to Violet. Chase was all man and he scared her more than any other man she'd encountered—

even Shawn. Shawn was all smooth sophistication, but Chase—he was hard and rugged.

When Chase's brief tutorial on the next phase was over, the crowd scattered leaving London standing alone with him. "Do you need my help?" he inquired when he saw her still standing there.

"No, no, I got it."

"Good." Chase turned his back on her and walked away.

Was this the same man who'd come to her restaurant requesting a second chance? It didn't appear so. He was seriously giving her the cold shoulder and London wasn't at all sure she appreciated it. Was that his MO? Play hot and cold and see which one worked best? Well if that's the way he wanted it, he'd be waiting a long time.

The rest of the day continued in the same vein, with Chase supervising the volunteers' work. But he wasn't above hard work himself; several times, London caught him lending his back and arms to get walls, roofing, and the porch done or just helping when a volunteer was struggling.

London hated to admit it, but Chase was good at being the leader. That's probably why Matt had put him in charge of this house while he helped managed the house next door.

By the end of the first day, the house had been buttoned up and was water-tight. Tomorrow, they would finish up the home's electrical, plumbing, and more. London was looking forward to seeing another home completed for a deserving Katrina survivor.

"What do you say to drinks at the bar?" someone shouted as they all headed to their cars.

"Sounds good to me." Several voices echoed that sentiment.

Next thing London knew, Violet was driving behind a caravan of cars, trucks, and SUVs heading to the Wishing Well of all places.

"You don't mind stopping for a drink, do you?" London

asked Violet from the passenger seat. "I know it's been a long day."

"No, I could use a drink after all that back-breaking manual labor."

London frowned. "It's for a good cause."

"I know, I know. Lighten up, London," Violet teased as she parked the car in the bar's parking lot at the rear of the building. "You're wound up as tight as a knot."

"Am not."

"Are to. And you and I both know why."

"Why?"

"Two words: Chase Tanner. The man has you all kind of hot and bothered. I've never seen someone get under your skin like he has."

"I'm not hot and bothered. I just don't appreciate being stalked."

"You know the man didn't stalk you. He hasn't paid much attention to you at all today, which is probably why your panties are in a twist."

"I couldn't care less who Chase gives his attention to," London responded.

Seconds later, she was eating those words. Once they went inside, London saw several attentive Habitat for Humanity female volunteers surrounding Chase at the bar. Her stomach knotted up.

Violet bumped her shoulder. "Told ya, you're green with envy."

London ignored the dig and headed toward the bar for a much needed cocktail. Violet joined her and soon she was laughing and talking with other volunteers about the day and what they liked or hated most. She was trying to get her mind off Chase and onto something else, but that was proving futile. She desperately wanted to turn behind her and find out what he was up to, but her pride forced her to put on a performance like she was having the best time.

After nearly an hour, Violet stifled a yawn. "Girl,

I'm tired. Do you mind if I retire? We have another long day tomorrow."

London wasn't ready to go, not with Chase still here. She had to show him that he hadn't gotten to her. "Can't we stay for a bit longer?"

"I'm going to fall over if I don't get some rest, then I'd be a liability tomorrow. I'm sure one of the volunteers can take you home."

"*I* can take her home," a masculine voice said from behind them.

London's stomach twisted. Slowly, she spun around and when she did, she came into direct contact with Chase. He was mere inches away from her and she could smell the musky scent of his cologne and feel his breath on her skin. "I-I... don't need a ride. We can go now." She turned back around to Violet.

Violet glanced back and forth between the two of them. "Oh, I want no part of this," Violet responded, stepping backward. "Stay, hash it out. Kiss. Screw. Or do whatever it is you two need to do. Otherwise the sexual tension between you is going to combust." Violet gave them both a salute and headed toward the door.

In disbelief, London watched her friend leave. Had she just told her to kiss or screw Chase? Lord! Sometimes Violet was just *too* much.

"Quite frankly, I like either of those two suggestions," Chase said, cutting into her thoughts.

London rolled her eyes as she glared at him. "I just bet you would, since you've been trying to get me into bed from the moment we met."

"Without much success, I might add." Chase leaned against the bar and stared back at her.

"Perhaps you're going about it the wrong way."

Chase stood up straight. "Is that right? Then let's try something else." He grasped her hand, placed both their beer bottles on the bar, then led her to the small wooden dance floor just as a slow song came on.

34

"What do you think you're doing?" London asked when Chase's arms encircled her waist, bringing her into close contact with the hard expanse of his chest.

"I'm doing what feels good," he whispered in her ear. "Now put your arms around me, woman, and enjoy the moment."

London was stunned by his honest answer. She wanted to push away from him and run, but another part of her wanted to know what it would be like to be *this* close to Chase. And so, she did as he instructed. She wrapped her arms around his neck and let him sway their bodies to the music.

She could feel her face becoming heated and her heart... well it was beating a mile a minute, faster than she could remember in a long, long time. And Chase was the reason for it. She could feel the hard ridge of his abs as he pulled her closer to him. Could feel the strong muscles in his arms as he held her. For the briefest moment, she allowed herself to wonder what he would look like without any clothes on.

Immediately, she glanced down, not wanting to look up at him, but Chase didn't allow it. One of his arms remained encircled around her waist, while the other was free for him to use. He forced her chin up with his free hand so she'd have no choice but to look at him. His dark eyes bore into hers. What she saw there was real, raw lust. Undisguised. Her lips parted, parted of their own volition. Her eyes closed and she titled her head.

That's when Chase's lips met hers, causing heat to flash throughout her entire body like lightning. His kiss was firm yet steady. And when he opened his mouth so his tongue could lick the seam of her lips, London allowed him entry into hers.

He kissed her long and deep while his hands moved lower from her waist so he could grip her tightly against him. He groaned and whispered, "Why do you keep fighting me?" His lips left hers to trail a path of wet kisses to her neck, where he gently nipped her with his teeth.

London was so caught up in the moment, she had to have him repeat it. Her brain was fighting against itself. "Wh-what did you say?"

"Why do you keep fighting what's between us?" Chase asked, pulling away from her slightly. "You and I both know there's something here. You feel it and I feel it."

London sighed. She hated herself for succumbing to the moment. "What I know is that you're obviously a man who's used to getting what he wants." She pushed away from his chest. "And you want me, that much is obvious. But the thing is, Chase, I want more."

"How much more?"

"A lot more. More than you're probably used to giving," London said and stalked off the dance floor.

Chase caught up to her in two long strides. "I'm not capable of more than that, London. You have no idea what I've been through."

"Yeah, well, I've been through a lot too, Chase. So has the rest of the world. You don't have the monopoly on hurt."

"Why can't we just have fun and see where this goes, London? What's the harm in that, huh?"

He made a good point. London wasn't ready to jump into another full-blown relationship either. She needed to regain her own footing and see who she was outside of being Shawn's wife. Chase was offering her a good time. What was wrong with that? "I need to think about it," London said. "In the meantime, are you going to take me home or what?"

Chase smiled. "Of course I'll take you home."

Fifteen minutes later, Chase pulled into London's driveway. During the short ride over to her home in Mid-City, Chase had hoped that London was giving some serious thought to spending time with him.

Back in the bar, when he'd held her and they'd shared one helluva kiss, he'd felt her desire for him. He'd also felt her resistance. As much as she tried to act like she was unaffected by him, he knew otherwise. She'd not only enjoyed the kiss he'd initiated, she'd kissed him back. Now he just had to build on that until their relationship came to the inevitable conclusion: London in his bed.

"Thanks for the ride," London said, reaching for the passenger handle.

"Can I walk you to your door?"

"I don't think that's a good idea," London replied. "You might try to angle for an invitation inside."

Chase held up his two fingers. "Scout's honor. I won't try for an invite." That didn't mean he wouldn't try to steal another kiss from the full-figured beauty. When they'd been in the bar, he'd finally gotten a chance to touch her, to feel all those delicious curves spill over in his hands, and he wanted more. Hell, he wanted all of it, but he'd have to wait until later.

Exiting his truck, Chase walked over to the passenger side and helped London out of the car. When they walked up the steps, her porch lights came on. "See, I'm home safe and sound, you can—"

He didn't let London get another word out. Instead he closed the distance between them, forcing London backward until her behind was up against her door. Then his lips moved over hers, deepening the kiss. A low moan escaped from London, giving Chase the entry he needed inside her delicious mouth. The foreplay of their mouths, lips, and tongues in a mating dance caused Chase's shaft to grow.

He forked his hands through her hair and tilted her head, allowing him to adjust their position. He cupped her butt and pulled her to him so she could feel the hard line of his shaft. She rocked her hips against him, causing a low feral growl to escape his lips. Kissing London was the best and worst kind of torture. Chase wanted so badly to make love to her, but now was not the time.

With all the strength he could muster, he gently pulled away. Both of their breathing was labored, but he managed to say, "You think long and hard, London, about whether you want to explore what I'm offering. But know this: I won't give up trying to convince you."

Chapter 4

*P*OW. POW. POW.

Chase fired back at the target they'd been trying to hit since they arrived in Afghanistan. The sound of gunfire erupted around him. He struggled to see through the smoke to find his comrades in his platoon, but he couldn't. The smoke was too intense. The smell of death was in the air. He coughed uncontrollably, but he couldn't breathe. He was going to die here. He had to get out. He had to get out now while he still could.

Chase bolted upright. Foggy, he blinked, trying to focus on his surroundings. He wasn't in the desert. He was in his bedroom in his New Orleans apartment, where he'd moved to six months ago. He glanced at the clock on his nightstand. It read three a.m.

Damn! He'd had another dream. The same one he'd had since leaving that ungodly hellhole and coming back home to the United States. But it wasn't a dream. It was a nightmare that had actually happened to him. He and his platoon had gone in, guns blazing, to take out a terrorist militia cell. They had met with heavy resistance and a grenade that took out half their platoon, leaving Chase and a handful of his team alive to tell the tale.

He'd rallied and gathered those he could and gotten them to safety. As Sergeant First Class, that was his job—to protect those under his command—but he hadn't fully lived up to it. He'd lost five soldiers that day and their faces lived on in his dreams—faces of the men whose wives, mothers, and sisters would never see them again. He'd promised to protect them and he'd failed miserably. That deployment had been his last of the six he'd done before putting in for his retirement. Of course, it was a little too late for his marriage, because after ten years of being married to an Army man, Bianca had moved on. She wanted someone with higher rank and privileges who wouldn't be on the front line like Chase.

But did she have to choose his mentor? The one man he'd looked up to his entire career?

That hurt.

Barefoot, Chase climbed out of bed and headed into the kitchen for some water. He'd thought he could deal with the nightmares, but they'd been coming more often lately, and were more vivid, more real. It was like he was right back in that rat-infested desert with no place to turn.

Reaching for a glass from the cupboard, he turned on the tap and drank directly from the faucet. He had to pull himself together. He wasn't one of those men who would use PTSD as a crutch to say he couldn't work or go on with his life. He was a man, a strong man, and he wouldn't let it beat him down—not now, not ever.

Later that morning, he was glad to arrive at the Habitat for Humanity site and be around other people. During the brief counseling he'd had when he'd returned to the States, the therapist had told him it was good for him to get out. Told him he needed to re-engage with society.

Well, he was doing just that and there was one person in particular that he wanted to engage with.

He watched London and Violet as they worked with several men to install windows and doors in the home. It wasn't as easy as it appeared, but London was game. Chase liked that about her—that she wasn't above hard work or manual labor. Most of the women he'd hooked up with wouldn't be caught dead with a chipped fingernail, much less get dirty. They were the high-maintenance types. Was that why he was so drawn to London, because she was different from the other women he'd dated?

She was certainly thicker, with wide hips, a large ass, and those breasts. Last night, when they'd kissed and her breasts had pressed against him, his shaft had grown large in anticipation of what he'd like to do to them. Kissing her had been fantastic and he couldn't wait to do it again.

"Chase, you wanna help with tarring the roof?" one of the men asked him, breaking through his thoughts.

"Nah, you go ahead and tackle that," Chase said. Of all the tasks in building a home, roofing was his least favorite. He didn't mind building the roof tresses as he'd done yesterday, but tarring and shingles were not his thing.

He found another way to make himself useful and headed straight for London.

She and another volunteer were struggling with putting in a window in the right position. They kept failing at the task. Chase stepped between them, taking the window from London and together he and the volunteer installed it in place.

"I had that," London sniffed from behind him.

Chase glanced backward at London, who had her hands on—in his opinion—ample baby-making hips. "Well, it looked like you needed a hand."

"We did," the man beside him said, nailing in the window.

Several minutes later, they were done, but when Chase looked up, London had already walked away to help out on another project.

"Is that your partner?" the man asked, following Chase's gaze.

Chase chuckled. "No, but I'm trying." The day was far from over and he would find another way to spend more time with London.

London went inside the home to find Violet, who was with the electrician completing the rough-in. "Need some help over there?"

"No, I got this," Violet said. "I thought you were installing windows."

"I was until Chase came over like some caveman to help little ol' me. Do I look feeble?"

Violet laughed as she glanced up at London's sour expression. "No, but he was probably just trying to get with you after last night." London had called and woken her up, much to Violet's chagrin, to share that she and Chase had kissed not once, but twice.

"Well, I'm not trying to *get* with him."

"Why don't you go help the plumber with the rough-ins?" Violet asked, annoyed by her response. "I'm busy here."

"Whatever!" London wrinkled her nose at her friend and went off in search of another task. Unfortunately, the plumber already had help from other volunteers. She bumped right into Chase as she exited one of the home's two bathrooms. "Are you following me or something?"

"In case you hadn't noticed, this is a twelve-hundred-square-foot house and is pretty small. There's not a whole lot of wiggle room."

"I know that, so what else can I do?" London inquired. "Violet's busy with the electrician."

A large grin spread across Chase's lips and London's stomach somersaulted. "The insulation crew is almost finished. We can go behind them and start the drywall."

London shrugged. As this point, there was no escaping Chase's company, so she might as well give in to it. "Alright." She followed him into one of the bedrooms that had already been insulated.

"You see that plasterboard right there?" Chase asked, pointing to a stack of Sheetrock lying in the middle of the room. "Well, we're going to use that to cover up the insulation. Then we're going to tape it."

"What do you mean 'tape it'?" London asked. She glanced around her. "I don't see any tape, only buckets of mud."

Chase laughed. "We're going to cover all the cracks and nails that we nail down the drywall with—that bucket of mud as you call it. We need to make sure the walls are completely smooth for when it's time to paint."

"Let's do it."

After Chase walked her through how to install the drywall, London was ready to do it on her own. They were a good team. Chase with his brawn would haul the drywall to the location and London would use the nail gun to secure it in place. They continued working in tandem until the entire room was done.

Then they stepped back to observe their handiwork.

"Pretty damn good!" Chase said and offered London a high-five, which she readily accepted.

"Thanks." She was proud of herself. "What's next?"

"Let's mud it. Here, let me show you."

He walked over and grabbed a bucket of spackle and brought it over to where London stood. "You see these nails. I want you to put a layer of spackle over them, but not too much." He stood behind London and slid his arms around her with the spackle and smoothed some of it onto a nail in the wall.

London held her breath. *What the hell is he doing?* "I thought you were supposed to be showing me how to mud a wall?"

"I am," Chase whispered in her ear just before his tongue reached out to lick her earlobe.

"Ah," London hissed and sucked in a breath as Chase's arm pulled her backside firmly against him. She could feel his growing hardness behind her as his hot, wet tongue licked and flicked at her earlobe. It felt *so good*. London knew she should pull away, but she was powerless, especially when his tongue darted inside her ear. She moaned aloud and her head fell backward against his shoulder.

"Ahem," a lough cough came from the doorway. Embarrassed, London sprang away from Chase. Thank God it was just Violet and not another volunteer seeing her behave so wantonly.

"I was wondering where you were, but it looks like you found another task more enjoyable. I'll leave you to it."

"Violet!" London called after her and tried to move, but one of Chase's arms encircled her waist.

"Don't go!"

"Why, so you can feel me up some more?" London asked as she fled the room.

She caught up with Violet at the front door. "Violet, wait!"

Violet smiled broadly. "Hey, don't let me stop your fun."

"It wasn't like that."

"C'mon, London, who are you fooling? That man is hot for you. And from the sounds I heard escaping from you, the feeling is mutual."

London grasped Violet's arm and pulled her aside on the porch, out of earshot. "Must you talk so loud?"

"You didn't seem to mind back in the bedroom where anyone could have walked in and saw you guys making out."

London sighed. Violet had a point. How could she be upset with her when she herself was to blame? She'd allowed Chase to treat her like an object and hadn't pushed him away. "I'm sorry, okay. I don't know what's wrong with me. He has me on edge."

"More like on fire."

London rolled her eyes at her friend. "Perhaps we should leave."

"And when have you ever walked away from something you believed in?" Violet asked. "Don't start now. You wanted to make a difference, so do it! Get out of your own head and finish what you started."

London heeded Violet's words and for the rest of the

afternoon, she kept her focus on the task at hand: finishing the house. They made great strides and by the end of the day, the house was nearly done. The subflooring and air-conditioning units had been installed. The electricians and plumbers were finishing their last fixtures and the millwork company was installing the cabinetry and countertops.

"I can't believe how quickly this all came together," London said as she and Violet looked up at the home. They'd add one final coat of mud, and their work on the project would be done.

"Shows what hard work can do," Violet replied. "Thank you for including me. I really enjoyed it."

London smiled. "No, *thank you.* I know you're not one for manual labor, but you really dug deep on this one."

"Can I get in on the action?" Chase asked, coming behind them and circling his arms around both women.

"Oh, you stink." Violet removed his arm from around her.

Chase laughed. "Well, you're not smelling all that wonderful yourself, toots, but my stench will be well worth it when the family moves in."

"That's right," London concurred. "Well, I've gotta go. It's back to the grind tomorrow." She started toward her car. She'd driven herself and Violet over today because she wanted to make sure they were on time. "See you around, Chase."

"Oh you can count on it." He gave her a wave as she slid into her Jeep.

"See, that wasn't so bad, once you focused," Violet said from the passenger seat.

London stared at Chase, who was still standing in the middle of the yard watching her. "Yeah, it wasn't, but I can assure you, I haven't seen the last of Chase Tanner."

Chapter 5

"H EY, BABY GIRL, WE MISSED you at church yesterday," London's grandfather said when she stopped by his home Monday afternoon before heading into the restaurant. He was sitting outside on the porch swing reading a book.

"I was volunteering at Habitat for Humanity. We were building a new home in the Ninth Ward."

"That's my girl, always lending a hand. So what brings you by?"

London had come because she'd needed some sense of normalcy after the weekend she'd had. Being near Chase for two days had worn on her nerves. She was antsy and jumpy because she never knew when he might sneak up on her, like he'd done yesterday numerous times on the job site. After the kiss in the bedroom, he was coming behind her and grasping her arms to show her proper home-building techniques. That's what he'd said, but London knew better—it was yet another way for him to get close to her. He'd continued to do the same thing for the entire day.

"Oh, can't a girl come by and see her grandpa?" London inquired, sitting beside him on the swing. "Do I have to have an ulterior motive?"

"Nope." He shook his head. "But I think you do."

"It's nothing really," London said.

47

"C'mon, it's me you're talking to, London—your grandpa. You know I can read you like a book."

London smiled sideways at him. That was true. She'd never been able to get anything by her very observant grandfather.

"There's this man—"

"Say no more," Grandpa Jeremiah interrupted. "I don't need to know your business."

"Grandpa." London laughed. "It's not like that. He's just different, is all. I have a hard time telling if he's truly genuine and on the up and up."

"How so?"

"One minute he's coming on strong. The next minute, he's volunteering at Habitat for Humanity. I can't reconcile the two men."

"Why do you have to?"

London turned to him. "What do you mean?"

"He's the same person. There's just two sides to the same coin. When he's with you, he's one way, but that doesn't mean he can't have a heart and can't help others."

"I suppose. I just can't figure out if he's friend or foe."

"Sounds to me like you know the answer, but you just don't want to believe it."

"Hey, how'd you get to be so wise?"

He chuckled. "Well, I *have* lived forty years longer than you, my dear, and might know a thing or two." He changed the subject. "So have you talked to your mama recently? No one's heard from her."

London shrugged. She and her mother didn't stay in touch. They were like oil and water and couldn't be more different. If she were more like her mama, she'd be jumping Chase's bones right about now instead of keeping him at bay. "Neither have I," she answered her grandfather. "You know Loretta doesn't stay in touch."

"You shouldn't call her by her first name. She's still your mama."

"Then you should tell her that because she hasn't been one in a long time."

"London—"

"Don't London me, Grandpa. She only shows up when it's convenient for her. Where was she when I was going through my divorce from Shawn? Nowhere."

"Me and your grandma were here and so was your aunt Ella."

"And I thank God for it because if you weren't, I'd have had no one. If you'd left me with her all those years ago, Grandpa, I would have grown up alone waiting for her to come home."

He reached for her hand and gave it a squeeze. "But you're not alone and never will be. I've got you."

"Thanks, Grandpa."

Chase couldn't get London off his mind. The attraction between them was palpable. He'd felt it a week ago in that bedroom when he'd been showing her how to mud drywall. She was just too scared to act on it. What made her so afraid? He wanted to know more about her and the only person who seemed to know her was her best friend, Violet.

Recruiting Violet to his side wasn't playing fair, but if London refused to acknowledge the simmering attraction between them, he had to use whatever means were at his disposable.

While they'd been volunteering last weekend, Violet had let it slip that London attended church regularly on Sunday. Chase was not a religious man. How could he be after all he'd done, seen, and endured during his time in the military? Instead, he should be begging God for forgiveness so he didn't go straight to hell for all he'd done in the name of his country and protecting its freedom. But he couldn't go back. Only forward.

That Sunday morning, forward led him to the Baptist church London attended. Dressing appropriately for the occasion wasn't easy. He didn't own many suits. He had less than a handful that he'd kept for funerals and Lord knows, he'd attended his share of those over the last twenty years. Nonetheless, he'd put on his best black suit with a lavender tie and now he was heading inside the sanctuary.

The service had already begun or at least the singing portion, so Chase sat in the back of the church and quietly sang along. He had to give it to them—the choir could really blow and he got into the mood. He didn't even mind the sermon because all he could think about was London.

He'd tried spying her out in the crowd, but it was too difficult thanks to women and their big Sunday church hats. When the service was over, he would wait for her outside and away from prying eyes. Church women had a tendency to be gossips, or so he'd heard.

Promptly at one p.m., the service ended and the congregation began spilling out. Chase stood off to the side but in clear view of the entrance so he could see London when she departed. He caught sight of her several minutes later when she exited with an older couple.

Chase nearly stopped breathing. She was a vision in a printed wrap dress that stopped just below the knee thanks to her height and showed a lovely expanse of leg that went out to low-heeled sandals. What really caught his attention was her hair. It hung in luxurious crimped waves down her shoulders. He'd never seen her wear it this way and he liked it. He liked it a lot.

As if she sensed him from the stairs, her eyes connected with him as he stood on the lawn under a tree. They narrowed into slants and not in the way he'd remembered when she'd moaned as he'd teased her earlobe.

He watched London whisper something to the elderly

couple right before she began stalking toward him. He prepared himself for her wrath.

"What are you doing here?" she hissed when she reached him.

"To hear the Lord's word."

London rolled her eyes. "I highly doubt that."

"You doubt my sincerity?" he asked with a smile.

"Chase, this has to stop. You can't keep showing up everywhere I go."

"Today, yes, I admit I came here to see you," Chase replied, "but last weekend was not planned. I've been volunteering for Habitat for Humanity for many years since I served in the Army."

"You're ex-military?" she inquired. "My grandfather is a veteran."

"You could find out more about me if you agreed to go out with me," Chase said. "There's a lot more layers to peel." London gave him a small smile. "Omigod! There it is. A smile." He pointed to her dimpled cheek. "I didn't think you knew how with me around."

"That's because you infuriate me."

He laughed. "I think I do more than that, but I'll leave that to another day. Join me for dinner *tonight*."

"I can't. I always have Sunday dinner with my grandparents, that's when I'm not at Shay's."

"Did I hear my name?" London's grandfather said as he led her grandmother over to where she stood with Chase under the tree. "And who do we have here?" He looked at London.

"Grandpa, I'd like you to meet Chase Tanner. Chase, this is my grandpa, Jeremiah Watson, and my grandma, Grace Watson."

Chase offered his hand to her grandfather. "Pleasure to meet you, sir. I hear you're a military man as well."

"Have you served?" London's grandfather asked.

"Yes sir. Twenty years, but I've retired."

A shocked expression crossed London's face and her grandparents'. Grandpa Jeremiah recovered first. "At your age? How old are you, son?"

"Forty-two."

"Mighty impressive, mighty impressive," Grandpa Jeremiah said. "Join me and the family for dinner. It's the least we can offer you after all your years of service."

Chase turned and looked at London. "Only if it's alright with the lady."

"O-of course, if that's what Grandpa wants," she replied.

Chase smiled broadly. "Would love to." This day couldn't have gone any better if he'd planned it. He'd get a glimpse into London's world and maybe she'd finally see he wasn't a scoundrel.

London couldn't believe how easily Chase had maneuvered an invitation to dinner. And through her grandparents no less! His persistence was annoying *and* flattering. Clearly, he saw something in her that Shawn hadn't. Shawn had found it easy to go outside their marriage bed and sleep with someone else. Afterward, London's self-confidence and esteem had plummeted. Had she been lacking physically and sexually? Is that why he'd chosen a prettier, slimmer woman?

Having Chase so interested was certainly a confidence booster. Maybe she really did have what it took to keep a man not only interested, but chasing after her. Or that's what she tried to tell herself as she drove behind her grandparents to their home. She could see Chase in her rearview mirror. She thought about trying to lose him in traffic, but that would rile him up more.

Maybe once they had dinner together—even with her grandparents present—he could see that they weren't compatible and keep it moving. Or so she hoped.

When they arrived at the homestead, Grandma Grace

immediately went into the kitchen to check on the roast she'd had in the crockpot. Meanwhile, London, Chase, and Grandpa Jeremiah made themselves comfortable in the living room.

London's grandfather took a seat in his usual armchair across from his wife's matching armchair. London sat on the couch and Chase joined her there.

"Thank you for having me over, sir," Chase said. "It's unexpected, but appreciated. I've been trying unsuccessfully to get your granddaughter to agree to join me for dinner."

London turned to glare at Chase. *What is he thinking, telling my business to Grandpa?*

"Is that right?" Grandpa Jeremiah asked, smirking at London. "So tell me, Chase, which arm of the service were you in?"

"Army."

"Me too. And you said you served twenty years?"

"Yes sir. Initially I did five years in the Army before I was recruited to be in Special Forces."

"So you did the year of schooling required for Special Forces?"

Chase nodded. "Was pretty grueling, but yes I made it through."

"Impressive." Grandpa Jeremiah rubbed his chin. "What made you decide to leave?"

Chase paused for several moments before he finally said, "I served my time, sir. I did six tours and spent a lot of time away from my wife... ex-wife that is. Cost me my marriage. It was time for me to go."

Grandpa Jeremiah nodded in understanding. "I appreciate your honesty."

Chase sat up straight on the couch. "Honesty. Integrity. Loyalty. Those are all words I live by."

London was stunned as she sat beside him. There was a lot more to Chase Tanner than she'd believed and if it weren't for her grandfather she would have never realized this.

"I'm going to go help your grandmother in the kitchen." Grandpa Jeremiah rose from his chair. "You make sure Chase here is comfortable." He patted London on her shoulder as he left.

She stared as he walked away. She'd never known her grandfather to so much as offer a helping hand in the kitchen, let alone leave her with a man in his house, but that's exactly what he'd just done. Had Chase really made such an indelible impression on him that he would leave the two of them alone? Apparently so.

All her manners went right out the window and London folded her hands in her lap, unsure of what to do next, so she asked a nonthreatening question. "Why did you stay in the Army so long?"

Chase laughed. "Is that really what you want to ask me?"

"No." London hazarded a glance at him and when she did, she connected with his dark-brown eyes. She swallowed and then scooted away. "So, you're divorced?"

He turned around so he could face her and threw one arm over the back of the couch. "Yes, as are you."

"How do you... don't tell me. Violet?"

Chase smiled broadly. "Guilty as charged. Don't be upset with her. She only wants the best for you."

London's brow rose. "And that's you?"

"Could be. But you'd have to go out with me to find out."

"Why should I bother? You seem to be doing such a good job of convincing everyone around me that you're the next best thing." London jumped off the couch. She paced the room, stopping in front of the fireplace. "Do you know my grandfather has never left me alone in the room with a boy before?"

"A boy?" Chase chuckled. "No, I suspect he wouldn't trust you alone with one of them." He rose from the couch and followed her to the fireplace. "But a man. Yes, I think

54

he might trust you with a real man." Chase reached for her hand and brought it to his lips.

London snatched her hand away. "Stop that, you're confusing me."

"I'm not trying to confuse you, London. I thought I was making myself clear—I want to spend time with you."

"You mean sleep with me," she corrected.

"If it leads to that, yes," Chase stated unapologetically. "As I told your grandfather, I believe in honesty." He drew closer to her side and this time London didn't pull away from him. His face was inches from hers and London could smell his musky cologne and feel the heat emanating from his nearness. "I'd very much like to make love to you," he whispered in her ear, "because not much sleeping will be involved when we're finally together."

"You two ready for dinner?" Grandpa Jeremiah asked from the doorway.

London stepped away from Chase at the fireplace as if they'd been caught in flagrante.

Her grandfather smiled broadly. "Well, it looks like you two could both use a drink. Chase, what do you have?" He walked into the room and headed to his small wet bar in the corner.

"A Scotch if you have it."

"My kind of guy. And for you, London?"

"Nothing for me, Grandpa."

"I think you could use a spirit," he responded and poured all three of them a glass. When he was done he handed them each a drink.

London didn't want hers, but accepted it anyway.

"What should we toast to?" Grandpa Jeremiah asked.

"To your beautiful granddaughter," Chase said almost instantly.

London's grandfather beamed his approval. "To London."

The three of them clinked glasses.

Dinner went even more smoothly than Chase had hoped. Not only had he won over London's grandparents, but he was beginning to believe he might be charming the lady herself. London had warmed up to him quite nicely over dinner and dessert, which in Chase's opinion was the best peach cobbler with homemade ice cream he'd ever had. Her grandmother could burn!

They sat around the dining room table talking until eventually he rose from his chair. "Mr. and Mrs. Watson, thank you so much for dinner," Chase stated. "It's been a pleasure spending the evening with you."

"You as well, son," Grandpa Jeremiah said, joining him on his feet. "You'll come again soon?"

Chase glanced at London. "If your granddaughter doesn't mind the intrusion."

She graced Chase with one of her enchanting smiles and his gut clenched. Spending time with London made him feel like a schoolboy again.

"I don't mind," she responded.

"Then you'll see me again, sir." Chase pumped his hand in a shake. "London, will you walk me out?"

"Of-of course." She stood and Chase rushed over to pull out her chair while her grandparents watched them. With his hand on the small of her back, Chase led her from the room and into the foyer.

"Did you really mean what you said back there?" Chase inclined his head toward the dining room.

"Yes, I don't lie to my grandpa."

"That's good to know," Chase said. "Can I take that as a sign you've finally realized I'm not the devil incarnate and will agree to spend time with me. Alone." He added the last word for good measure because as much as he'd enjoyed London's folks, he wanted to spend time with London. Just the two of them.

"If it'll mean you easing up and not coming on so hard," London's voice trailed off, "then the answer is yes."

Chase smiled. Persistence was key and it had never failed him. "How about Friday night? My place. I grill a mean steak." He watched her visibly swallow as she mentally weighed her options. He wasn't going to give up or stop asking her out. The solution was to give in to him.

"If I agree and this date is a bust," London said, "will you stop asking me out?"

Chase laughed. "It won't be, but yes, I'll agree to leave you alone."

She smiled. "It's a deal."

Chase would love to have sealed it with a kiss, but out of respect for her grandparents, he let London walk him to the door and kissed the top of her hand. "Until Friday night."

Chapter 6

"I HAVE NOTHING TO WEAR," LONDON fretted as she stood in front of her walk-in closet, staring aimlessly inside. She hadn't done much in the last half-hour except complain.

"London, you've plenty of clothes," Violet commented. She sat on the edge of London's queen-sized bed as she watched her get ready for her date with Chase this Friday evening. "I bet I could find you something real easy."

London turned to glare at her. "I've gained weight. Thirty pounds since Shawn's sorry ass left me. Nothing fits."

Violet sighed heavily and rose from the bed. "Move aside." She pushed past London and began rifling through her closet. Within seconds, she pulled out some distressed jeans and a graphic T-shirt. "Wear this!" She handed London the hangers.

"These won't fit."

"You won't know until you try. Now stop complaining and get dressed."

Five minutes later, London stared at her reflection in the mirror. Violet was right and the jeans fit. Yet despite the fact she was wearing her most hip-hugging pair, she hated that her hips were overly wide. She wished she had the hourglass shape her sisters Jada and Bree had inherited.

Why had she even agreed to dinner with Chase? And

to his home no less? She knew he was only interested in the quickest way into her pants. She'd said yes to his invitation, if for no other reason than to get him off her back and maybe off her mind. Since she'd first met him, he'd enveloped her thoughts. And when he'd kissed her at the Wishing Well and brought her home, she'd nearly been on the brink of losing self-control and inviting him into her place.

"Are you nervous?" Violet asked when London remained silent.

"Maybe just a little."

"Don't be. It's obvious Chase is really into you. Why else would he go through the effort of finding out more about you through me?"

"Speaking of which," London said, spinning around on her size ten feet, "I have a bone to pick with you, missy."

"Oh yeah?" Violet puffed out her chest. "That I what? Actually helped the relationship along and gave you the push you needed?"

"You need to stop interfering."

"Well, someone has to help you because you clearly won't help yourself. Perhaps you should be looking at me like your fairy godmother instead of giving me hell. I only want the best for you."

"And you think Chase is it?"

Violet shrugged. "I have no idea, but neither do you. And you won't unless you spend some time with the man. And so what if it leads to sex. When was the last time you got any?"

London's brow furrowed. She couldn't remember the last time she'd had sex. She and Shawn had long since stopped having sex way before their divorce. That should have been her first clue that he was getting it from someplace else, but she'd figured it was because she'd gained weight.

She'd never been a size six even in her teens. She'd

always been a full-figured gal and when she'd met Shawn, she'd actually lost a few pounds because she'd been desperate to keep a man as fine as him. But her love affair with food had resumed once she'd snagged him and they'd married. She'd slowly started packing on the pounds she'd lost and then some. Perhaps it was because she'd never thought she was good enough for him to begin with.

After they'd married, she'd turned a blind eye, not seeing Shawn's transgressions because he'd been a practiced liar. It had been humiliating to learn how long he'd been deceiving her. But more than that, it made her feel foolish that she hadn't seen the truth from the start. It had been a bitter pill to swallow and the reason she was so reluctant to go down that road again. It was easier to live in spinsterhood.

"Don't remember the last time I had sex," London finally answered Violet's question. "I've closed up shop down there."

"Bullcrap," Violet replied. "You're only thirty-two and you're still a young, vibrant woman—same as me. And you have needs. Needs that a man like Chase can fulfill."

"Dammit, Violet." London glanced at her friend. "Are you wishing you had the date tonight?"

"Hell yeah," Violet said. "If I had a man like Chase chasing after me, I'd show you what I'd do with him. But he's not interested in me. He wants *you*. So go get your man."

Violet's words echoed in London's head as she drove to Chase's apartment in Uptown. At one point she'd been tempted to turn around and go back home, take a microwave meal from the freezer, and pop on Netflix in favor of facing her attraction to Chase. Isn't that what scared her most about the evening: that her body was responding to him in a way she hadn't known before? Something told her that being with a man like Chase was dangerous and it wasn't because he'd been in Special Forces.

Chase was excited for the evening to come. Matter of fact, he couldn't recall another woman he'd gone through all this trouble for. But intrinsically, he knew that London was worth it. Hadn't she shown that by all the hard work she'd done in building the Habitat for Humanity home? She wasn't one of those women who was all about the chase, coyly playing with him. London gave it to him straight. She wasn't afraid to tell him exactly where to go—which no other woman had ever done to him before.

But Chase was hoping tonight would be different.

He was hoping to show her a gentler side of himself as he'd done at her grandparents' place and that she'd be softer. He wanted her to let down some of the walls she'd erected.

He'd first attempt to achieve this by reaching her through her stomach. He'd been marinating Kona-flavored rib-eyes for the last twenty-fours and they would go on the grill once she arrived. He'd accompany them with bourbon maple mashed sweet potatoes—a dish he'd found online— after he'd served her a mixed green salad.

He was just putting the finishing touches on the salad when his doorbell rang. Wiping his hands on his apron, Chase walked to the front door. A large grin spread across his face when he saw London on the other side. "Hello, beautiful."

London was casually dressed in ripped jeans and a form-fitting graphic T-shirt with glittered cap sleeves and high-heeled sandals. The T-shirt showed off her ample breasts. Chase's mouth couldn't help but water at the prospect of diving into her bosom and getting lost.

She smiled back at him. "Chase." She handed him a

brown paper bag with what appeared to be a bottle of wine in it.

"Come on in." He opened the door as he accepted the wine. "You didn't need to bring anything, only yourself."

London walked inside his apartment and her tumble of curls fell over her shoulders when she turned and said, "My grandparents raised me with manners and to never come empty-handed as a guest."

He closed the door and stepped back for several moments to watch her walk away. He loved the way her hips sashayed from left to right. They were baby-making hips that could withstand a man as strong as him pounding into them.

Chase swallowed. He had to get his mind out of the gutter. London would bolt if she knew the lascivious thoughts running through his mind. Instead, he followed behind her and found her in the living room, glancing around at his sparse furnishings.

Through her eyes, he could see his apartment looked far from lived in. The walls were devoid of pictures or paintings and the room was sparsely decorated with a couch, coffee table, and an entertainment center that housed a sixty-inch television.

"Make yourself comfortable," he said as he headed to the kitchen across from the living area. He liked that the open floor plan allowed him to watch London from afar without her noticing.

She did as he asked and sat down on the sofa while Chase went about making himself useful by opening the bottle of wine she'd brought. "I hope you don't mind cups," Chase said as he used the wine opener he'd found she'd brought in the bag. Thank God she had because he certainly didn't own one. He was used to a brewski after a long day's work.

London swiveled around on the couch to look at him. "Not at all. It all goes down the same."

"I'm afraid I don't drink wine much," Chase said and poured them both some into two red plastic cups. "Never acquired the taste for it."

Instead of waiting for him, London rose from the sofa and came toward the kitchen. "Don't much myself. Except what I learned from Shawn." She quickly covered her mouth. "I-I'm sorry. I didn't mean to bring up my ex."

"Don't apologize," Chased replied, handing London a cup. She accepted and quickly took a sip of wine. "I imagine he was a big part of your life, so it would be natural for you to bring him up in conversation. How long were you married, if you don't mind my asking?"

"Five years."

"Long time," Chase replied. "And no children?"

London shook her head. She'd wanted children, but Shawn had been reluctant to start a new business and a family. Then she'd started gaining weight and, well, he'd had other ideas.

Chase groaned inwardly. Had he said the wrong thing? "I'm sorry. That was inappropriate."

"It wasn't," London responded. "After five years of marriage, most people would have expected children, but it wasn't in the cards. And you?" She took another tentative sip of her wine. "How long have you been divorced?"

"Not quite two years. But really it was probably long before that since I was deployed on and off during our marriage and hardly saw Bianca."

"Do you regret that?"

He stared at her. No one had ever asked him such a pointed question. "At times, yes I have. But I've come to realize that she wasn't the woman I thought she was and her duplicity would have eventually come to light."

"Sounds like you've done a lot of self-reflection."

"I've had nothing but time." Chase took a sip of wine and immediately wished he could spit it out. Wine was definitely not his cup of tea. Nor was the direction this conversation was taking. When he'd thought about having London in his home for dinner, it certainly hadn't included a walk down memory lane and rehashing his divorce. "How about I put the steaks on?"

"Sounds good. And if you don't mind, I'd love a Bud Light." London placed her cup on the counter. "This wine is horrible. The man at the liquor store said it was good, but it's too dry for me."

Chase grinned. London was his kind of gal.

Out on Chase's apartment patio, London sighed as she leaned against the railing and watched him turn the steaks over on the grill. She was surprised when she'd arrived and found him wearing an apron, of all things. She'd thought he would have gone to his favorite takeout eatery and ordered them some dinner. She hadn't expected that he'd actually cook for her or that the smells coming from the grill would make her stomach growl.

"Those steaks are smelling divine," London commented.

Chase glanced up at her from the grill and grinned proudly. "Coming from you that's high praise."

"Though I have to admit I'm surprised that you're cooking."

Chase walked over to her from the grill. "I had to do something to impress you."

"Impress me?"

"C'mon, London." Chase closed the distance between them until he had her pinned between him and the railing. "You know you haven't exactly made getting to know you easy."

"Perhaps if you'd never come on so strong..." Her voice trailed off.

"I would have stood a chance?" Chase surmised correctly. How was it that he could read her mind?

"Maybe."

"And now?"

"Now what?"

"Do I stand a chance?" He leaned forward into her personal space and stared deep into her eyes. She saw his eyes gleam and knew he was determined to persuade her otherwise.

London straightened, afraid of what she saw. "That remains to be seen." She stepped away from him, giving herself some much needed distance. "Would you like another beer?" she queried as she headed toward the patio door.

"Sure."

Chase watched London escape into the safety of his apartment. As much as he wanted her, he could see the wariness lurking in her eyes. Her ex-husband had done a bang-up job of destroying her confidence and trust in her instincts. She didn't seem to realize that her body was betraying her. Her nipples had tightened underneath her graphic tee, telling him she was just as sexually excited as he was and it was a futile exercise to run. His groin beat with anticipation of what he was sure would come to fruition between them. It was just a matter of when.

He removed the steaks from the grill and placed them on the rack he'd brought outside, then made his way for the kitchen just as London, holding two bottles of beer, was about to exit it.

"Steaks are done," he said as they ran into each other.

"What can I do?" asked London, who abandoned her plan to head outside.

Stand there and let me stare at you, Chase thought. But instead he said, "You can help me set up the table. Dishes are in the cupboard." He inclined his head toward the cabinets behind him.

London set the beers on the rectangular table in the eat-in dining room between the living area and kitchen.

When he finished arranging the steaks on the platter, getting the potato casserole out of the oven, and grabbing the salad from the fridge, he placed his masterpieces in the center of the table.

London had set up their beers next to two place settings, which gave Chase the line of vision that would allow him to look across at her all evening.

"Mmmm, smells delicious," London said as she leaned over the table and breathed in the scents. As she did, her breasts rose and fell and Chase got an instant hard-on.

"Let's dig in." Chase came around to pull out her chair for her.

"Thank you," London said.

Chase reached for her plate at the same time as London did, and in that instant, an electrical current shot through him *and* London. He knew they'd shared the current, because London's eyes darkened when she looked up at him. London knew the current was reciprocal too. Chase added a steak and potatoes to her plate while she busied herself tossing the salad that didn't really need it. When she was done, she added a generous helping to her plate. Chase took his seat at the table.

Chase liked that she wasn't afraid to be herself and eat around him. He hated going to dinner with women who picked at their food and was glad London wasn't one of them.

He watched her cut into the Kona-flavored steak and waited for her reaction. When she placed the delicate piece of medium-done steak into her mouth, Chase wished he was on the other end of the fork as it swiped her generously full lips. When she was finished chewing, he asked, "Well?"

A large grin spread across her pink-tinted lips. "It's divine, Chase. What rub did you use on it?"

Chase laughed. "Well, if I told you I'd have to kill you."

"C'mon." London cut off another piece of steak as he did the same. "You have to tell me your secret."

He shook his head. "Not unless you coerce me." He would love nothing better than for London to use her feminine wiles on him.

"Maybe I will," she responded playfully.

In Chase's opinion, the rest of the evening went smoothly— not only with dinner, but later when he played the saxophone for her, much to her surprise. He hadn't played in years, but there was something about London that relaxed him and made him feel good.

And throughout the night, they talked about how London started her restaurant and why Chase had joined the military. This line of conversation led him to regale her with some of his tales abroad... or at least those he could share that weren't classified.

"You've led a pretty remarkable life," London said. "You've traveled around the world, unlike me."

"You haven't traveled?"

London shrugged. "Not unless you count here, Texas, and a honeymoon in the Caribbean. That's not to say that I haven't wanted to travel. I would love to go to France and Italy and discover their cuisines."

"You would love it," he replied. "Once you've tasted pastries in Paris or a zuppa di pesce in Italy, you'll think you've died and gone to heaven." Chase rolled his eyes upward.

London laughed. And Chase liked the sound of it. She was relaxed and finally letting him see a side of her she probably kept hidden from the world.

"What?" she asked when he continued to stare at her.

Chase shrugged, reached for his beer, and took a swig as he regarded her. "I just like this side of you."

"Don't like it too much," she responded.

"Ah," he said, pointing to her with his pinky finger, bottle still in hand, "there's the prickly London I know, but I've already seen the vivacious one and I like her even better."

"Chase..."

He didn't say anything. Instead he rose from the table and started clearing off the dishes. He didn't want to move too quickly and spook her or she'd run off. He was enjoying her company too much to let that happen. He began washing up the dishes and London sidled up beside him.

"You don't have to help," he said.

"It's no problem." London used the hand towel tucked in the refrigerator handle to begin drying the dishes.

"This is nice," Chase said. "Spending time without sparring."

London raised an eyebrow. "Sparring? Yes, it does seem to come naturally to us."

"And you know what they say," Chase said as he scrubbed a pot.

"And what do they say?"

"That love and hate, or is it lust, are just different sides of the same coin."

"And which of those do you think we fall under?"

Chase dragged in a deep breath. He knew the answer and knew she knew it too. So why were they playing this game? He dropped the pot back into the soapy dish water and closed the distance between them. He grasped London by the shoulders and her head fell backward, her lips slightly parting.

"What are you doing?" she managed to utter. He hauled her firmly to him until their bodies fit in perfect unison, just like two puzzle pieces. She gasped just as his head descended and his mouth took hers. He kissed her softly at first. Her lips were a touch sweet from the bourbon maple mashed sweet potatoes and Chase groaned, deepening the kiss, testing her to see if she was as hungry and needy as he was to taste her. To feed the dark craving he'd had of this woman since the moment he'd seen her across the crowded bar. His shaft grew in response and he knew

London *felt* him, but she didn't pull away from him. So he kissed her again, long, hard, and deep.

Her arms ensnared around his neck and Chase backed her up against the sink. He anchored her head into the crook of his arm so he could fully explore her mouth, her sweetness. He used the tip of his tongue to flicker across hers and London met him stroke for stroke.

Chase could feel desire coursing through his veins and one of his hands moved from the small of her back upward to cup her breasts through the T-shirt. He rubbed his fingertips across one of her breasts and her nipple puckered beneath his touch. Chase would love nothing better than to lower his head and take the engorged bud in his mouth, but was London ready?

She was certainly moving the lower half against his throbbing erection. Chase took a chance and without hesitation, he lifted London off the floor but didn't stop kissing her. She would have no choice but to wrap her legs around him if she didn't want to fall. Next thing Chase knew, he felt her legs circling around him.

Satisfied there was no denying what would happen between them, Chase, with London astride, headed down the hall toward his bedroom.

London was drowning in the silken web of desire that Chase had cloaked around her with each of his drugging kisses. She recalled kissing him in the kitchen and how the feel of his tongue on hers had sparked a desire in her she hadn't known existed. And then, Chase was carrying, *carrying* her to his bedroom. She had to be at least two hundred pounds, but he didn't seem to care. He *wanted* her and that knowledge caused any doubts London may have had about herself to disappear.

She wanted Chase as much as he wanted her. There was no denying that.

When Chase reached his bedroom, he deposited her on the bed and then left her long enough to flood the room with light.

London bolted upright. She'd never had the lights on when having sex. "Turn it off."

"Why? I want to look at you. *See* all of you."

"Just turn it off, for me, *please.*"

Chase heard the imploring in her voice and did as she instructed, then he returned to the bed. He covered her body with his and when London felt his hard, muscular form, she relaxed again.

Chase planted soft kisses across her lips, cheeks, and chin, and London's head fell backward as he trailed a path of tiny kisses along her ear and her neck. "You're beautiful," he whispered in her ear.

When she stilled beneath him, Chase looked into her eyes and before she said otherwise, he responded, "I mean it."

Then he kissed her again with an urgency that took London's breath away. Soon his hands were touching her everywhere and when his fingers found hers, he entwined theirs together as he rubbed his erection against her.

When he eventually lifted his head, he whispered huskily, "Do you see how turned on you make me?"

"I feel it," London responded.

Chase smiled. "Then let's do something about it." He rose on his haunches and reached for the edge of her T-shirt, whipping it over her head. His eyebrows shot upward when he saw the satiny red bra she was wearing.

"Did you wear that for me?" His palm caressed her breasts through the soft fabric and tweaked her nipple with his fingers.

Had she worn it tonight hoping the evening would end up like this? She'd always loved lingerie and having nice undies. It was one of the things that Shawn had always liked about her—that she had matching underwear. But she didn't care about Shawn anymore. She only cared about what Chase thought.

"Maybe subconsciously I did."

Chase's mouth glimmered into a smile. "Then I wholeheartedly approve." He reached for the front clasp on the bra and released it, allowing her D-cup breasts to spring free of their confines. His eyes lit up with appreciation and London's insides melted.

Cool air hit her skin, and seconds later she felt his hot mouth on her as he began sucking her. It had been too long since anyone had taken the time to worship her body. Most men wanted to get to the main course, but Chase seemed intent on taking his time, like she was a fine wine to be savored.

He nipped and grazed her nipple with his teeth and London released a low whimper.

"I like that you're vocal" Chase commented, glancing up at her hooded lashes. "Always tell me if you like what I'm doing. Or if I'm not doing something that pleases you."

London was surprised that he cared for her pleasure as well and not just his own. But all she could do was merely nod because while his mouth paid homage to her breasts, first one and now the other, his other hand had gone to the seam of her jeans and was caressing her between her thighs.

"Ahh," she cried out.

"Does that feel good?" he asked.

"Y-yes…, but—"

"But what?"

"You're driving me crazy," London muttered.

Chase gave her a wicked smile. "Well, that's the point. I want to drive you crazy until you come in my mouth, with me inside you. I'll take whatever I can get."

London was floored at how he was speaking to her. She'd never been one to talk much during sex, but Chase was different. He wanted to *know* she was enjoying every part of their lovemaking.

Wrapping her arms around his neck, she kissed him again and Chase took the hint and lowered the zipper on her jeans. Then he tugged the denim from her hips. Once freed, she heard his sharp intake of breath as he caught sight of the matching bikini bottoms.

"So beautiful." His hands circled her belly, almost rhythmically until he reached the triangle of dark curls at the apex of her thighs. London moaned when he pushed aside the panel of her bikini to finger her. "Chase, please..." Molten heat was spreading through her veins like wildfire. And when Chase slid a finger inside her ever slowly, London thought she would come apart.

It was exquisite torture having his fingers play her like a piano. He knew every chord to strike a response from her. She was a bundle of nerve endings, but Chase didn't seem to care—he was intent on making her a quivering mass of limbs. His fingers surged in and out of her moist heat and London thought she might faint from the pure pleasure of it all, but instead she came. Hard. Very hard. She let out a harsh cry.

Her cry was more strained when she felt Chase's mouth *there*. He was licking up her juices and teasing her sensitive flesh with quick flicks of his tongue.

Sweet Jesus! What is he doing to me?

London's nails dug into his shoulders in protest but Chase continued his quest, tonguing her with feverish delight until she came again in as many minutes.

"I think it's time I got as naked as you," Chase said and rose to strip.

London was liquefied on the bed. All she could do was watch Chase as he removed his clothing. His body was every bit as perfect as she imagined it would be. His chest was broad and his abs were ripped thanks to years of constant conditioning in the military. Add the trim torso, rock-hard behind, and the splendid evidence of his arousal, which hung long and thick, and London was eager to have him buried inside her.

Chase reached past her to the bureau by the side of his bed and produced a box of condoms. He'd been prepared for what he thought would eventually happen between them. And hadn't she known as well? That first night in the bar, she'd felt an instant attraction before he'd gone and muddied the waters.

But Chase had redeemed himself, showing her that he was more than that one moment.

As a result, she welcomed him with open arms back into her embrace and his head lowered as his mouth came back down on hers. He kissed her so passionately that any residual reservations she may have had skittered out the window and instead she allowed herself to feel. Every cell in her body was alive with need. The need for this man.

He moved over her and she felt his shaft nudging at her opening. "Look at me, London," Chase urged.

Her eyes had fluttered closed, but Chase was intent on living this moment with her. So she opened her eyes as he thrust deep inside her. A low gasp escaped her lips.

Chase looked down at London. Damn she felt good. She'd clamped around him nice and tight. And wet. So wet. He wanted to thrust deep inside her until he reached the hilt, but he needed to take this slow. Make it last for them both. They'd waited too long. He would hold back his release for as long as he could until he was sure London had gotten hers.

He concentrated on kissing her, fondling her breasts, the curve of her hip, her ass. And oh what an ass it was. He loved a woman with a big behind and London had enough for him to grab a hold of when he rode her hard. Because he intended to do just that, real soon.

Slowly, he began thrusting into her. In and out. In and

out. He felt London's hands on his sweat-slicked back, felt the tension in her thighs and need for him to go faster. But he wouldn't. He was focused on her. Her orgasm. He'd been with a lot of women and knew when they were reaching their climax.

London was near hers. She angled her pelvis as he began driving into her.

"Yes, Chase, oh yes, baby," she urged him on.

Chase gripped her hips and drove into her harder, faster, and soon he felt her spasm underneath him. As the full force of her climax hit her, she arched off the bed... and Chase rode her harder. He was going to fuck her through her orgasm... and he did.

His hips pounded into her over and over.

"London!" Chase groaned out her name as his own release washed over him and he collapsed on top of her still quivering body.

What the hell! What kind of spell had London put over him? He felt more alive than he had in years.

Chapter 7

L ONDON STRETCHED, ROLLED TO ONE side, and let out a deeply contented sigh. She felt languid. Sated. She didn't want to move from Chase's bed. He'd driven into her, making wild passionate love to her. London hadn't known sex could be this way, this *consuming.*

But she also didn't know what to do next. She hadn't come over to Chase's apartment intending to sleep with him. Sure, she'd worn her fanciest knickers on the off chance of an encounter like they'd had at the bar and outside her door nearly two weeks ago. Still, she'd never imagined she would end up naked in his bed with his muscular arm strewn across her, firmly holding her to his side.

His lids were shut and London imagined he might have fallen off to sleep as most men did after great sex. Now would be the moment to make a fast getaway before either of them had to deal with any awkwardness in the morning.

Slowly, London slid her large body from under Chase's arm and sat upright. She was about to rise when he tugged her down and flat onto her back.

"And where do you think you're going?" he asked. His dark eyes were staring into her brown ones. His gaze was filled with something akin to raging lust.

London fumbled. "I-I..." She couldn't think of a thing to say. Not when he looked at her that way.

"Were you going to slip out of my bed without a kiss goodbye?" Chase said.

London blushed.

"I don't want you to go, London."

"You don't?" Her voice sounded small, even to her.

"No, I don't. In fact, I'm not finished with you. We've just gotten started."

London felt the swell of Chase's erection at her hip and watched as he reached for another condom to protect them. Seconds later, he was scooting her beneath him and covering her mouth in a hungry kiss.

She gasped at the intensity, and the parting of her lips gave Chase the entry he need to draw the tip of her tongue into his mouth. Then he blew her mind by sucking on her tongue, hard and voraciously, reawakening her body and making her writhe underneath him.

Chase caught her hips and plunged hard and deep, burying himself inside her. He pulled her hard against him until her nipples rubbed against the hair on his chest. London's breath caught in her throat as he circled his hips while his mouth and tongue continued to devour her. He stroked his rigid length inside her over and over until she was dizzy with feverish delight.

"Yes, Chase, just like that," London moaned, not caring about the sounds that were escaping her mouth.

He continued teasing her until she was making sounds in what was akin to a plea for him to make her come. He obliged only when she convulsed around him—only then did he allow himself to let go and give a ragged shout of release.

Gunfire erupted all around him along with never-ending sirens. Chase crouched down in the tent as sand whipped around him in a frenzy from the impending sandstorm. He

tried to remain low, but he couldn't. He was sucking in sand because he couldn't find his protective mask.

Fear coursed through him. If he didn't find his mask soon, he would die of asphyxiation or some biological agent the Taliban was using against the United States Army. In his search, Chase crawled along the sandy floor, hoping he'd find his mask in time.

He did.

And once he had it on, he looked around for his men, hoping they'd be just as lucky, but there wasn't time. There was an explosion and all Chase saw was blinding light. His ears rang.

"Ahh!" Chase screamed, bolting upright in his bed in a cold sweat.

"Chase? Chase? Are you okay?" a soft feminine voice asked from his side.

Chase glared at her.

"Chase, it's me, London."

He blinked several times, trying to escape the nightmares and demons of the past and focus on the present. When his vision finally cleared, he saw London beside him in his bed. She looked extremely concerned.

"Are you okay?" she asked when he brought her into focus.

Nodding, he threw back the covers and jumped from the bed to head to the bathroom. He shut the door behind him and immediately rushed to the sink to splash cold water on his face.

Dammit! He was having one of the many recurring nightmares that had plagued him since he'd left that godforsaken desert. Most nights, he couldn't sleep because of the memories. They always came to him at night when he couldn't escape them. They would haunt him until the wee hours of the morning until eventually he'd give up the ghost and either fall asleep or get up. Usually he got up.

He was used to dealing with very little sleep. He'd been conditioned that way in the military.

Some nights, when exhaustion finally claimed him, he'd sleep like a log. Tonight, he'd almost made it through the night because of London by his side. *What must she think?* He was sure he'd woken up screaming or something equally as unattractive. She was probably outside the door getting dressed and hauling ass from his place as fast as her high-heeled sandals could take her. And could he blame her?

He was a hot mess.

Reaching for the hand towel on a nearby rack, he wiped his face free of sweat and reluctantly opened the door. Sure that he was facing an empty room, he walked out naked.

The room wasn't empty.

The bedside lamp was on, and London was sitting upright in the bed with his pillows bunched behind her.

He stopped midstride. "Hey."

"You look surprised to see me," London said.

"I kinda am," Chase said. "I can't imagine it's very sexy to have your lover hollering in the middle of the night and scaring the shit out of you."

London gave him a small smile. "I'm fine," she responded. "I'm more worried about you. The nightmare you were having must have terrified you. You were screaming."

"I don't want to talk about it," Chase said, walking to the other side of the bed and climbing in. "Can't we just go back to bed?" He reached across her and turned off the lamp. He wanted this conversation to be over.

"No." London turned the lamp back on. "Clearly you're upset, Chase. Perhaps you *should* be talking about it to someone. Maybe you'd feel better."

"London, please," Chase implored. "Can we talk about this in the morning? I don't want our first night together to be about *this.*"

She must have sensed his anxiety because she stared at him for several seconds before leaning over to turn off the lamp.

As she slid back down onto the pillows, Chase wanted to rid his mind of the memory. He only wanted to think about London and how she made him feel, so he took her hand and moved it between his legs.

"Chase."

"Stroke me, London," he whispered as he leaned in and licked her ear with the hot flash of his tongue. She did as he instructed and her fingertips lightly stroked up and down his length. "Yes, like that, baby, but harder, faster," he urged.

When she felt him close to the brink, London moved from beside him to astride him. She eased down onto his pulsing shaft and began to ride him. She knew what he needed and rocked her hips back and forth. His palms possessively cupped her bottom, eager to maintain the contact, but London was just getting started. She changed rhythm, easing up and down his length.

"London, babe," Chase moaned. "That's it, baby. Give it to me." He leaned upward and grasped her breasts in his palms. He sucked on them greedily. He needed her. He needed this. He needed to forget. And she met his every need.

Her body quickened around him and Chase lost all control. He shouted out his release.

Chase awoke to the smell of coffee and bacon. Wiping the sleep from his eyes, he glanced to the side of the bed and saw that London's soft frame wasn't there. After they'd made love for the third time last night and London's bottom had curved into his middle, Chase had finally fallen into a deep sleep. This time with no dreams.

He glanced at his clock. It read nine a.m. That was late

for him. He never slept in. His body was his own alarm clock, but not this morning. London had an appetite for sex that matched his own. She'd shown passion and agility during their lovemaking. Whoever said full-figured women didn't know what to do in the bedroom was truly mistaken. London knew exactly how to get him off, be it with her hands, her mouth, or her body.

Rising from the bed, Chase pulled on some jogging pants that had been lying across the room in a nearby chair. Then he padded toward the direction of the delicious scents wafting from his kitchen.

As he walked down the hall, he heard the radio in the background. When he arrived, he found London dressed in one of his T-shirts. It barely reached her midthigh. She was gyrating her hips in tune to the music as she flipped pancakes on the stove. She was midcircle in her dance when she caught sight of Chase leaning against the wall admiring the view.

London stopped in her tracks and put her hands on her hips. "See something you like?"

"Hell yeah," he responded with an unabashed grin, walking toward her. He pulled her into his embrace and captured her lips. She responded and wrapped her arms around his muscular shoulders and he deepened the kiss.

After several moments, she pulled away and pushed against his chest. "Don't start something we can't finish," she responded. "I have pancakes to watch." She bumped her generous hips against him and returned to the stove to check on the food.

"And I can't wait to have some."

He didn't have to wait long. Shortly afterward, London finished making breakfast and they sat at his breakfast bar on the wooden stools he'd bought at a garage sale. Somehow the woman had whipped up a veggie omelet of broccoli, carrots, and onion from his refrigerator's sparse contents. The blueberry pancakes that accompanied the omelet were divine.

"That was delicious," Chase commented when his plate was empty. He leaned back in his seat and regarded London. "I'm amazed you were able to find something to make."

London shrugged. "It's a gift you pick up when your mother leaves you in the house without grocery shopping. You learn to make something out of nothing."

Chase noted the hurt tone in London's comment. "I take it you don't get along with your mother."

"That would be an accurate assessment," she responded curtly. "The only person Loretta Watson cares about is herself. Having a child was always unwelcome."

"I'm sorry." Chase reached for London's hand, but she pulled it away. "Let's talk about something else," he said.

They did just that. Chase filled London in on his family. He told her he was born and raised a Texan and that his mother passed from a drug overdose when he was six years old. He'd moved in with his single father, who'd raised him.

"Myles Tanner knew nothing about raising a kid," Chase revealed, "but between the two of us, we figured it out together. He was always there for me and I knew I could count on him, including my decision to join the Army when I was eighteen years old."

"Why so young?" London asked, sipping on her coffee.

"Considering where I grew up in Waco, Texas, I didn't want to go down the drug dealing path and end up in jail, but I also wasn't too keen on books and college, so my only choice was to go into the military. 'Cause my father made it real clear that he wasn't having a grown man sitting up in his house, eating his food, and mooching off of him like some black mothers allow their sons to do."

"Sounds fair," London said. "Where's your dad now?"

Chase's face turned somber. "He passed away when I was stationed in Germany. I was only twenty-three."

"Oh Chase!"

He shrugged. "I was able to make it here and say my goodbyes. That's all I can ask."

London stared back at Chase, amazed at all he'd done and been through and the fact that, despite it all, he was still standing. Losing both his mother and father when he was so young, it was tragic. And here she was complaining that her mother was MIA. At least Loretta Watson was alive.

"You're very resilient," she finally said. "I guess that's why you're able to handle the nightmares too. How often do they come?"

Chase grimaced. He was hoping London had forgotten the incident. He'd certainly tried to change the conversation by sexing her like crazy, but apparently it hadn't worked.

"Not often. Listen," Chase said, standing up, "this is something I really don't feel comfortable talking about."

"I can see that," London said softly, "but if you're hurting—"

"London," Chase hissed through clenched teeth. Why was she pushing the envelope? Why couldn't she leave well enough alone?

"Chase, you can't keep—"

She never got to finish because Chase raised his voice and yelled, "I said enough!"

London dropped her napkin on the plate and rushed out of the room. Chase stared down the corridor. *What the hell have I done now?*

By eleven a.m., when she'd finally made her way to Shay's, London was still shaken up about the night and morning she'd spent with Chase.

On the one hand, Chase had woken up in her a sexual side that had been lying dormant. She'd always had a

84

high-sex drive, but Shawn hadn't been interested. Instead, he'd made her feel like something was wrong with her for wanting a sex life on the regular. He'd harped on her weight and the more he'd harped, the worse she'd felt and the more she ate. Finally, he'd gotten her wish and she didn't want to have sex nearly as often. She'd felt fat and ugly and far from sexy. But thanks to Chase, last night she'd felt sexy and desired. It was an exhilarating feeling, almost like she was on drugs. It was a high that she could definitely get used to.

On the other hand, the sexual fire that had crackled between them had quickly fizzled when London pushed him to open up about the nightmare he'd had. She was certain it wasn't his first and probably wouldn't be his last, but Chase was putting his head in the sand and refusing to deal with it.

But did his harsh treatment of her negate everything that had happened before? He'd made her feel beautiful and cherished. She'd felt more alive, wilder, hotter than she'd ever imagined she could be. How could she make sense of it all?

London chose to focus on the positive side of their time together and the amazing chemistry they shared. A smile returned to her face as she prepared orders on the line for the lunch rush.

"And what's got you so chipper?" Charlotte inquired as she rolled dough on a floured surface for a batch of fresh biscuits.

"Me?"

"Who else?" Charlotte asked looking around. "You're beaming like a neon sign."

London blushed and her light-brown skin turned red. "Oh no reason, I just had a good night."

"Would it have anything to do with that handsome

specimen that was here a few weeks ago who sat at a table all night waiting for you?"

London stopped and turned to stare at Charlotte. "How'd you know about that?"

"C'mon, London." Charlotte laughed as she continued to work on the biscuits. "This is a small establishment and we all gossip. Not to mention, we're all family."

London smiled. It was the culture she'd wanted at the restaurant. During their marriage, Shawn hadn't agreed and felt there should be a clear delineation between the management and staff, but London wasn't like that. She liked that her staff shared life's ups and downs with her and that they knew she cared about them. To her, it made for loyal employees.

"Well..." London paused several beats. "If you must know, it does. We had a date last night and it went great."

A large grin spread across Charlotte's face. "That's wonderful, London. I'm so happy for you. And if you don't mind my saying, it's about time. I know you and Mr. Shawn were together awhile, but you never seemed happy. At least not how you are now."

Long after the lunch rush had ended, Charlotte's words resonated with London as she sat in her office going over the purchase orders for the week. *Had it really been obvious to everyone that I was unhappy with Shawn?* She'd always tried to put up a good front, but clearly the cracks had shown.

Her cell phone vibrated on her desk. Glancing down, London frowned at the display but answered anyway. "Hello."

"How's my girl?" Duke Hart asked from the other end of the line.

"I'm fine," London replied to her father. "How are you?"

"I'm good," he said.

"But?" London heard the hesitation in his voice.

"But nothing. How's business?"

"C'mon, Dad. I doubt you truly called to find out how Shay's is doing." They'd never had that kind of relationship where she shared what was going on in her life. That was reserved for Grandpa Jeremiah. He was her confidant. Duke Hart was her biological father—nothing more, nothing less.

"Would it really be so bad if I were?" Duke inquired. "Honestly, London, I'd like a better relationship with you. Know more about what's going in your life."

"Like you do with Bree and Jada?"

"Quite, frankly, yes," Duke answered. "I know I didn't get to raise you like I did your sisters and that's always been the single biggest regret of my life—not knowing of your existence."

London released a heavy sigh. "We can't go back, Duke."

"I know that," he said, "but can't we go forward? Can you make room in your life for me?"

London thought about Duke's request. There was so much water under the bridge, too much time had passed. She wasn't sure it was even possible to form a relationship with Duke this late in the game. And she wasn't sure she wanted to try. Why get her hopes up about a father-daughter relationship like she saw in the movies? That dream had died long ago for her.

"London?" Duke broke into her thoughts.

"I don't know."

"I appreciate your honesty."

"I don't want to give you false hope, Duke, that we'll ever have what you have with Jada and Bree. You knew about them from the moment they were born. You loved their mother."

But he didn't love hers. That was the unspoken truth lying between them. Duke Hart had impregnated Loretta after a drunken one-night stand. He didn't learn of

London's existence until years later. Of course, ignorance didn't him make not liable for being a father, but London was sure he'd felt he had a pass.

"I admit your mother and I weren't lovebirds," Duke responded, "but that doesn't mean I don't love you or Trent any less."

Trent.

He was London's younger brother by another one of Duke's one-night stands, sired while Duke was married to Abigail Hart, Jada and Bree's mother. Except Trent's mother had known exactly who she was bedding and made it clear to Duke that he would do right by her son. So Trent had always known Duke Hart was his father, whether he liked it or not. In Trent's case, he and Duke were like oil and water. They didn't mix.

"How is Trent?" London asked.

"Up to no good," Duke replied. "Same as usual."

London hated that at twenty-seven, Trent could never seem to find his way. He'd dropped out of college to work on an oil rig and aimlessly went from one job to another. She suspected Trent had thought he'd run Duke's oil company, Hart Enterprises, one day, but that job had gone to London's cousin Caleb Hart. After giving up bull riding and chasing women, Caleb had joined Duke's company and Duke had taken him under his wing. He and Duke were made from the same cloth. London envied him.

"Sorry to hear that," London finally commented about her brother.

"Enough about everyone else," Duke said. "You always want to change the subject rather than talk about yourself."

London smiled. She'd always been that way. "Not much to speak of. Business is steady, but could always be better."

"And your love life?"

"What of it?" London asked defensively.

"Whoa there, girl. I was just inquiring if you were seeing someone special, but if you don't want to share—"

"It's not that." London wasn't ready to share too much about Chase. Their relationship was so new and she had no idea where it was leading.

"Then what?"

London sighed. "There is this guy," she started. "It's a little early yet, but it's promising."

There. She'd gotten it out.

"That's wonderful news, baby girl. I know it's been difficult for you since Shawn."

How would he know that? London wondered. She certainly had never discussed her relationship with her ex-husband with Duke. "Yes, it was, but that's over and done with now."

"Glad to hear it. Well, listen, I have to run," Duke said, "but Jada and Bree will be visiting real soon."

"Good to hear from you, Duke. We'll talk soon." London ended the call and placed her cell back on the table.

It always surprised her when Duke called. Theirs was not the average relationship, but he seemed like he really wanted to remedy that. London just wasn't sure if she could let go of the past hurts and resentments she felt for his lack of presence in her life during her formative years. Perhaps one day she'd be able to forgive Duke and have the bond she always desired.

Chapter 8

C HASE WISHED THE EVENING WITH London could have ended on the high note on which it began. He'd had lots of bravado going into the evening, but deep down he'd never dared imagine that it would actually happen, that he and London would actually have sex. But they had, and it was one of the best nights of his life.

London was not only a smart, savvy businesswoman with a big heart—she was sexy as hell and a passionate lover too. She'd been warm and receptive to his touch and had given back in spades. Chase couldn't remember the last time a woman had excited him in bed. He'd had lots of willing females in his past, but none who'd touched him as London had. He wondered if she'd been self-conscious about her size and if that had made her shy toward him initially. But once she'd let down her guard, she was open and responsive to him, in and out of bed.

And then the nightmare happened.

Chase's lips twisted into a frown.

He'd tried pushing the incident aside and London had been gung-ho about his distraction method when he'd asked her to touch him. The way she'd moved up and down his length, working him to paradise and back again... she was everything a man could dream for, but she hadn't forgotten as he'd hoped.

When she confronted him that morning, badgering

him to talk about his feelings and the nightmares, he just couldn't take it. He hated that he'd snapped and raised his voice at her after the incredible night they'd shared, but she'd given him no other recourse.

And now Chase was unsure of what to do next.

Usually his connections with women were brief, a temporary fling. None of those other women had ever truly touched his life; but something in Chase sensed that London was different. There was something about her that settled him and made him feel at ease when they were together. And a part of him couldn't wait to have the tigress back in his bed to wrap her luscious, soft body next to his hard one.

But there was another part that told him to run and not look back. He was used to being free and unencumbered and London wanted to have a long-term relationship. Chase wasn't sure he was ready for that after Bianca; but if anyone could make him want more, it was London.

But being with London would come at a steep price he wasn't sure he was ready to pay. She would press him on his PTSD. If he stayed with London he would be forced to look into a mirror he'd rather turn away from. Was being with London worth the sacrifice and hell he'd have to endure to be with her? Chase needed time to figure that out.

"Why is it I have to come all the way to your place of business to get the scoop on your date last night with Chase?" Violet inquired later that afternoon when she stopped by Shay's. The restaurant was closed for a few hours, and London was wiping down and resetting the tables along with other staff in preparation for the dinner rush.

London looked up from a table in the middle of the restaurant and laughed at her friend. "I'm sorry, girl," she said with her hands on her hips. "The morning got away from me and once I got here, we were swamped."

"That's no excuse," Violet said as she helped London set up the salt and pepper shakers along with the napkin holders. "I want d-e-t-a-i-l-s. So spill."

London stopped her busy work and turned to smile broadly at Violet. "The evening was an unmitigated,"— London paused for effect and saw Violet's eyes widening in horror—"success."

"London!" Violet smacked her on the arm. "Don't do that to me. You were about to give me a heart attack."

London chuckled. "I'm sorry, I couldn't resist." She pulled out a chair from one of the tables and gestured for Violet to sit.

"I want to know everything from beginning to end," Violet said, taking the seat.

"Well, Chase cooked me dinner at his place: steak and bourbon maple mashed sweet potatoes," London replied. "Then he played the saxophone. We laughed and talked for hours, girl. I couldn't believe how well it went."

"And?"

"And after I helped Chase clean up, one thing sort of led to another and we ended up in bed."

"You what?!" Violet shrieked.

London glanced at the kitchen doorway. "Lower your voice. I still have staff in there getting ready for dinner service."

"You want me to be quiet after you drop a bombshell like that?" Violet sat back in her seat and stared at London. "I truly can't believe it. You? Miss Take It Slow-and-Easy? *You*, who said you were just going out with Chase so he would stop harassing you."

London shrugged. "Yeah, well, I'm a woman and I have needs. All of which Chase met in spectacular fashion. Over and over and over again."

"Ooh-wee." Violet fanned herself with her hand. "Is it getting hot in here or what? Was he that good?"

London could feel her face becoming hot and her cheeks turning red as she blushed at the memory of just how good Chase was. "That and then some."

"Well I ain't mad at you. If I had a fine specimen like Chase sniffing around me, I'd give up the cookie too."

"Violet, you're a hot mess, you know?"

"Yeah, well someone has to give it to you straight. When are you meeting him next?"

London stared back at Violet. Although they'd shared an amazing night in bed together, after Chase had raised his voice during breakfast, things had sort of gone downhill. She'd rushed off to the bathroom in his bedroom to get cleaned up, and when she'd exited, he'd been sitting on the bed waiting for her. It had been awkward between them. He'd walked London to the door, kissed her on the forehead and that had been the end. They didn't talk about seeing each other again.

"You mean he didn't ask about a second date?"

"N-no, he didn't," London responded with a slight quiver. "Is that bad?" She knew he hadn't been too happy with her pushiness that morning, but would he consider their entire night a bust? She certainly didn't. She wanted to see Chase again, which is why she chose to keep the details of the morning's event to herself.

Violet shook her loose curls. "Not necessarily. Let's just see how the day goes."

London nodded. She sure hoped she hadn't been right about Chase from the jump. She'd hate to think that he would use their misunderstanding as an excuse not to see her again. Now that she'd been free with the goodies and Chase had gotten what he wanted, was he already on to the next woman?

"Chase, I have to admit I'm surprised to see you,"

Mason said when Chase stopped by his three-bedroom home unannounced.

Chase hadn't known he was going to Mason's specifically. He'd run his Saturday errands and was heading back home, *or so he thought*, when his car had headed in the direction of Mason's bungalow.

"I'm sorry. If now is not a good time, I can come back another day," Chase said. Mason was the closest person Chase had to a friend. Although they hadn't seen each other in years, after reconnecting again, their former friendship had been renewed. Chase saw Mason as a confidant.

"Man, you're here now," Mason replied, opening his front door wide so Chase could enter, "so stop playing and get in here. You must have something on your mind."

"Is it that obvious?" Chase inquired, stopping midstride in the middle of the living room, adjacent to the entrance.

Mason shrugged. "Maybe not to some, but we go way back." He inclined his head toward the rear of the home. "C'mon back to the kitchen."

They stopped long enough for Chase to give Mason's wife, Kelly, a hug and kiss before Mason led him outside and into the garage.

"Welcome to my man cave." Mason flicked on the wall switch and flooded the room with light.

Chase surveyed the place and liked what he saw. On one wall loomed a sixty-inch television with a large comfy sofa in front of it and a popcorn machine. Tucked in the corner but facing the TV was an enormous beast of a treadmill along with a punching bag suspended from the ceiling that ensured Mason kept his retired military body in shape. But if Chase were honest, what he appreciated most of all was the bar setup across from the entertainment area. It looked like it held an assortment of liquors along with a mini-fridge.

"You've quite the setup."

"I know." Mason smiled broadly as he reached inside

the fridge to produce two bottles of beer. He handed one to Chase. "Have it just the way I want it and Kelly can't say a thing because it's my space. You know, out of sight, out of mind."

"Happy wife, happy life." Chase accepted the bottle. He unscrewed it and then tipped it in Mason's direction.

"So, not that I'm not happy to see you or anything, but do you want to tell me what brought you by?" Mason took a swig of his beer. "Or should I guess? A woman perhaps?"

When Chase turned to stare at him, Mason knew he had his answer. "Is it the plus-sized gal you've been talking about?"

"How you'd guess? And does her size matter?"

Mason snorted, "Of course not. She's the only female you've been coming on strong to. So is she still not giving you the time of day?"

Chase had shared with Mason that London had been less than receiving of his previous attempts to get to know her. He was sure Mason would be shocked to learn just how intimate their relationship had become in the last twenty-four hours.

Chase finally shook his head in response. "No, she finally eased up. Oh and—"

"And what? Don't leave a brother hanging."

Chase was silent, not wanting to kiss and tell but by the same token, he was confused as to what to do next. He'd never enjoyed spending time with women unless they were underneath him, but London was different. She was the first woman in a long time to make him *feel something*— maybe even want more than his usual one-night stand.

Mason crouched down until he was eye to eye with Chase. "Did you hit that?"

Chase hated the crude way it sounded, especially when it came to London. She wasn't his usual hit-and-run chick. "It wasn't like that."

"Oh snap." Mason rose to his feet and covered one of his hands on his mouth. "You've finally been sprung."

"Sprung?" Chase stood. "It's not like that."

"Oh no?" Mason said, swigging his beer and taking a large gulp. "Like hell it's not. She put her swerve on you and now you twisted."

"Damn, Mason. I came here for a friendly chat, not to be roasted over the coals."

Mason laughed. "Relax, relax. That's exactly what you're going to get. But after the chicks you've hit it and quit it with, you have to admit that turnabout is fair play."

Chase shrugged. "I suppose." He began pacing the garage floor. "I didn't expect last night to go as far as it did. Did I hope? Of course, but it came as a shock to me as well. And it... it was different with London. Special, you know? She's not my MO. She doesn't sleep around, so—"

"She was feeling you too. That's good. So what's the problem?"

Chase released a long, heavy sigh. "The problem is, London is the kind of woman you get serious with."

"The kind you go beyond the surface with," Mason added for Chase.

"Exactly." Chase pointed his finger at Mason with his beer in hand. "And I thought I was ready. I'd been hounding her to give me a chance."

"And now you're running scared?"

"Hell yeah." He was afraid of screwing it up and making London regret ever becoming involved with him. "You know what I've been through, Mason. The life I've lived. The things I've seen. That I've done. I'm not sure a good girl like London is ready for all of this, all of me."

Mason nodded in understanding. "You have been through a lot, Chase, and that's exactly why you need to let go of the past and embrace your future. A future free of pain and regrets. You need to start looking forward."

"That's easier said than done."

"Do you still have the nightmares, the flashbacks?" Mason asked quietly.

Chase nodded. Years ago, Chase had undergone exposure therapy—a systematic process of confronting harsh memories—but he had quit it almost right away. Other than the military therapist he'd seen all that time ago, Mason was the only person who knew he suffered from horrific nightmares that made him wake up in a cold sweat. "I had one last night."

"When London was there?"

"Yeah. Scared the shit out of her, because I woke up screaming and didn't recognize her at first."

"That's not good."

"Don't you think I know that? I don't want her to fear *sleeping with me, being with me.*"

"You have to get some help, Chase. It's what I did. When I got back, I was a wreck. I was no good to Kelly. Loud sounds would make me jump. I was on edge all the time. One night after a really bad nightmare, I nearly choked her to death."

"Jesus!"

"Kelly left me the next day. Told me if I wanted our marriage to last, I needed to get my shit together or she was gone."

"And therapy cured you?" Chase replied, disbelievingly. He doubted that any amount of therapy could erase the image of seeing his comrades in pieces on the ground. Erase the sounds of explosions on a nightly basis.

"Not entirely. I'm still in therapy. Go once a week, but I'm a helluva lot better than I was before."

"That's all fine and good for you, but I've never believed all that mumbo jumbo and I ain't about to start now."

"So instead you'll condemn yourself to a life alone with countless females going through a revolving door? That's no life to lead, Chase. You must realize that or you wouldn't have come here for advice."

Chase rolled his eyes at his friend and took a swig of beer. "You know you talk entirely too much."

"And you talk entirely too little," Mason shot back. "Always been your problem. But if you intend to get serious with this woman, which it sounds like you want to do, you need to start talking to someone who can really help you... you need to start talking a lot."

London pulled her Jeep into her grandparents' driveway. Not that she wasn't happy to see them, but she had no idea why she was being mysteriously summoned to the house in the middle of the week. She was about to find out.

London got out of her Jeep and walked tentatively to her grandparents' door. It wasn't locked, and she walked right in. "Mama," London said when she entered the parlor and saw Loretta Watson sitting across from her grandparents.

Loretta was there for one of her infamous drive-by visits. She would stop in every now and again to do a pulse check to make sure everyone was still alive before she headed out to find another man to hang on to. Loretta Watson couldn't stand being alone.

"Is that the best greeting you can give your mama?" Loretta jumped to her feet and pulled London into a reluctant hug.

London glared at her grandfather, who merely shrugged. He knew she didn't appreciate the ambush. If she had her way, she'd forgo Loretta's visits.

When Loretta finally pulled away, she looked at London. "Girl, look at you. You just keep packing on the pounds. I told you, you'll never find or keep a man unless you drop some weight."

"Why, it's good to see you too, Mama," London responded, sitting in an armchair as far away as possible from her.

"Oh c'mon, London, don't be so touchy," Loretta said,

rolling her eyes. "I'm just trying to help you. Look at how well your mama keeps herself in shape." She motioned her hands down her body.

London eyed her mother. At fifty-four, with smooth cocoa butter skin, the woman had nary a wrinkle on her face. London was sure Loretta was easily a size six or eight in the leopard top and skin-tight jeans she wore. She would never dress her age and London had long ago given up thinking she would. She had to admit the woman knew how to keep herself in good condition; but it chagrined her to know that was only because she was a cougar who knew she had to look sharp while on the hunt for younger men. "You're looking well."

"You could too if you put some time and effort into it," her mother stated.

"Enough, Loretta," Grandpa Jeremiah finally spoke. "Why must you beat up on the child every time you see her?"

Loretta huffed, "I don't beat up on her, Daddy."

"No, you just put me down." London jumped up from her seat and headed to her grandfather's wet bar. Flustered, she poured herself a glass of Scotch.

"Do the same for me," Loretta requested.

"Of course," London said through clenched teeth. She made another drink and handed hers to her mother.

"So what's new, London? Catch me up," Loretta commanded. "Daddy told me you might be seeing someone new. When am I going to get a chance to meet him?"

Never, London thought. "It's too soon to tell."

Loretta took a liberal sip of her Scotch. "Oh don't be coy, London. Daddy says he's quite the catch, ex-military man and all. How'd you snag him?"

"Really, Mama," London said, rolling her eyes. It was completely inappropriate for her mother to bring Chase up in front of her grandparents. Further, London wasn't even sure where she stood with Chase. Since sleeping with him four days prior, he'd been MIA. London was wondering if she needed to send out a search party for him.

"Why is it so wrong to know what's going on in my daughter's life?"

"There isn't anything wrong with that," Grandpa Jeremiah replied, "but even you must realize, Loretta, that you can't pop in and out of London's life and expect things to be copacetic between you two. Not when you haven't worked at it."

"Dang, Daddy, I thought you were on my side."

"I'm on *both* your sides," he responded.

Loretta turned to look at London, who had sat back down in the armchair. "It's not my fault. I try to connect, but you won't give an inch."

"When have you tried, Mama?" London hissed. "When? The occasional call I receive after you've stopped dallying with one of your young playthings? Exactly when have you tried?"

"London!" Grandma Grace cried.

"See what I mean," Loretta shouted. "She's so disrespectful."

"That's because you have neither earned nor deserve my respect." London gulped the remainder of her Scotch and rose to her feet. "I don't know why you persist in showing up every blue moon when it's clear you care nothing about me. I have always been a hindrance to you, Mama. But guess what? You don't have to worry about me anymore. I'm a big girl and I can take care of myself. And when I can't, I lean on them," she said, motioning to her grandparents, who sat stunned on the couch at her outburst, "because they are the only family, the only parents, I have ever known or will ever need."

Without another word, London rushed to the front door and swung it open. Her grandfather stopped her before it closed. London had never seen him move so swiftly since perhaps when she was a youngster and had cut off her hair and he'd caught her to give her a spanking.

"London, was that really necessary? I have to agree with Loretta—that was completely uncalled for."

"I'm sorry, Grandpa, but I'm not going to act like there's not a serious problem with our relationship because Loretta wants to play Mommy every blue moon."

"Would it hurt you to try?"

"I have. For years, I've tried to give her the benefit of the doubt," London responded, "but when is enough enough?"

"She'll always be your mama."

London snorted. "Don't I know it."

"Is there anything I can do to help mend fences between you two?"

London smiled. "I wish there were, but you've done enough already. If Loretta wants more, she's going to have to put in the time and effort."

He nodded. "Alright, I won't press, but I'll see you on Sunday?"

"Of course. Wild horses won't keep me away." London attempted cheeriness as she closed the door behind her. As soon as she was in her Jeep and away from her grandparents', she pulled over to the side of the road and let out a loud sob. When would the pain of never having a mother hurt less?

Chapter 9

ON SATURDAY AFTERNOON, LONDON STARED down at her smartphone again for the umpteenth time in the last hour as she sat in her Jeep in the Fresh Market parking lot. It had been a week since she and Chase had slept together and she hadn't heard a single word from the man. Not only was she angry, she was hurt. *How could I have been so wrong?* Was her intuition so badly damaged after Shawn that she couldn't recognize when a man was using her for sex?

Because that's clearly what Chase had done, London thought. He'd gotten what he wanted and left her high and dry with egg on her face. She felt like a fool for trusting that he was on the up and up, that he wanted to get to know her and not just physically. Had her mother been right? Would she never be able to keep a man?

London put her phone in her purse, got out of her Jeep, and walked into the store. She was thinking about the choice words she'd have for Chase the next time she saw him when she ran into the man himself!

She had been sniffing some tomatoes in the fresh fruits and vegetables section when he saw his close-cropped head come into view.

Surely, it can't be him. But when a swarm of butterflies began to flutter in her stomach at the mere sight of the man's broad shoulders, perfectly accented in a fitted

T-shirt, and his strong thighs, which showed through his fitted jeans—she knew for sure it was Chase. London didn't imagine that a man like Chase actually shopped, much less cooked for himself, but if the basket he was holding, filled with protein shakes and bars as well as some boneless, skinless chicken was any sign, that's exactly what he was doing.

Her first inclination was to duck behind the onion and tomato bin, but why should she? She wasn't the one who'd said one thing and done another. She'd been upfront and honest about what she was looking for and he'd just been looking for a booty call. So instead of remaining silent, she did something completely out of character: She stalked over to where Chase stood fifty feet away. She glared at him until he looked up from the label he'd been reading.

His guilty expression said it all. He was busted! "Lon-London," he stuttered, "how are you?"

"Perhaps you would know the answer if you'd bothered to call me after the night we shared."

He grimaced. "I deserved that."

"That and a whole lot more," London responded. "What gives, Chase? You said you wanted to get to know me, but instead I get the silent treatment? No call, no text, much less any email in a week. But you know what? I'm good. I'm fine. I'm just dandy. Because now I know I was right about you from the jump and it taught me a lesson not to be so gullible the next time a good-looking man wants to talk to the fat chick. Have a nice life."

She spun on her heel to walk away, but Chase caught her arm.

"Don't touch me!" she hissed loudly.

Several nearby patrons turned to stare at them and he immediately let her arm go. "London, I'm sorry. You have every right to be angry with me. I handled this poorly."

Her eyes narrowed. "Ya think?"

"I know," he replied more firmly, "I owe you an apology."

London shook her head. "Don't bother. I don't need it. You showed me exactly who you are, Chase Tanner, and I don't want to hear any more of your lies. Go feed them to the next female."

She didn't wait for a response and instead began quickly walking to the checkout counter with the items she'd already had in her basket. Whatever else she needed, she'd have to buy another day. She couldn't bear to be in the same building with Chase, not after she'd made a complete and utter fool of herself.

"London, please wait!" Chase caught up to her at the checkout line.

Unluckily for her, there were several customers ahead of her, which meant there was nowhere to run.

"What, Chase? What?" London turned and glared at him. She felt her cheeks turning red. "What else do you want? Tricking me into bed wasn't enough for you?"

The customer in front of her coughed loudly, clearly embarrassed by London's outburst, but London couldn't care less. If she had to have it out with Chase right now, so be it. She wouldn't see any of these people again.

"London," Chase lowered his voice, so much so he was barely audible. "I'm sorry. Okay? I got scared."

"Excuse me?" London could hardly hear him.

"I said I got scared." His voice boomed so loud this time that the patrons and the cashier in line all looked in their direction. "Can we please talk privately?" Chase grabbed her elbow and pulled her out of the line.

"Why? So you can get me into bed again?" London replied. "I ain't that easy."

Chase shook his head. "No, so we can stop providing fodder for the Fresh Market employees and patrons."

"I have groceries." London held up her basket.

"So do I, but they can wait." He walked over to an empty aisle and set his basket down. Before London could object he took hers out of her hands and placed it alongside his.

Then he grabbed her hand and led her out of the store amidst the stares of several customers.

Once outside, London snatched her hand away. "Alright, Chase. We're outside. Talk."

"Coffee?" he asked. "There's a Starbucks around the next corner."

London folded her arms across her chest. "I'm not going anywhere with you, not ever again."

"Please don't be like this, London. It's not like you. Give me ten minutes—ten minutes of your time. Maybe then my behavior might make sense."

London stared at Chase for several long moments. Her head told her to get in her Jeep as fast as she could, drive away, and never look back. But her heart wanted to know why. Why hadn't he called her after they'd shared such an amazing evening and morning together? The chemistry between them had been thick enough to touch. Had it only just been London feeling like it was the best sex she'd ever had? The most connected she'd ever felt to another human being?

She had to know.

"Alright," she finally stated. "You get ten minutes. After that, I'm leaving."

"Fair enough."

They walked side by side in silence the two blocks to a nearby Starbucks. Despite it being well past lunchtime, the café was still bustling with activity. After ordering two coffees, they were fortunate to find a small two-seater in a corner by the barista. Chase's was black while London went for a calorie-laden Double Chocolaty Chip Frappuccino. She knew she should resist the temptation, but she always wanted comfort food or drinks whenever she was nervous or anxious. And she was definitely both. She had no idea what Chase was going to say.

Much to London's chagrin, Chase pulled out the chair for her and when he did she caught a whiff of his arresting scent. She hated that her traitorous heart did a flip-flop. She was happy when he finally took a seat across from her.

"Well?" London asked.

Chase took a sip of his black coffee and set it on the table. "I enjoyed the night we spent together, London, immensely as I'm sure you remember," he started. "I was, no—I *am* very attracted to you. Have been from the moment I met you, but I wasn't expecting the depth of how deeply I'd be touched by what we shared."

Memories of Chase shouting as he came inside her after they'd made love several times sprung to London's mind. She hadn't expected him to go for broke. London reached for her Frappuccino and indulged in a long gulp.

"You were right about me," Chase said.

London frowned. "How so?"

"Usually after I bed a woman, I'm out the door before morning. But it wasn't like that with you. I *wanted* you to stay. Wanted to make love to you again. Over and over again."

A rush of pink stained London's cheeks at Chase's blatant remarks.

Chase released a long sigh. "I do want more, London."

She snorted. "You have a funny way of showing it."

"I was afraid," Chase replied.

"Afraid?" London rolled her eyes. "You? Ex-Special Forces?" She sipped her frothy drink. This she had to hear.

"My fear has nothing to do with the physical. But I have been afraid of what could develop between me and you if I let it. If I let you see all parts of me."

London glanced up and this time her eyes connected with Chase's brown ones. And when they did, she was greeted by a naked hunger in his eyes. She licked her lips in an attempt to hide her nervousness, but her action caught Chase's attention and he stared at her mouth.

London's pulse began to skitter alarmingly.

She was right to sense danger because in one forward

motion, Chase was leaning across the table. His arm reached out to lock behind her head and pull her toward his mouth. London knew she should resist, but it was like she was watching herself in slow motion and was helpless to do anything but comply.

Instead, she allowed Chase to brush his warm lips across hers. The electricity of his kiss sent a delicious shudder running through her. But before she could enjoy the kiss, Chase pulled away, sat back down in his chair, and gazed at her.

"I know I shouldn't have done that," Chase said huskily. "I know I don't deserve to kiss you, much less ask you for a second chance, but that's exactly what I'm going to do. I messed up, London. I have a failed marriage behind me and a not so great record at relationships with women and enough baggage to fill up several dump trucks. I thought all that was enough of a reason to stay away because I didn't want to hurt you or get hurt in the process. But look at you, even after your divorce—you went out on a limb and put yourself out there. And I guess what I'm saying very longwindedly is that I'm willing to do the same if you'll give me another chance."

London stared back at Chase in shock. She hadn't yet recovered from his kiss even though his lips had touched her like a whisper. As much as she'd like to deny it, she'd wanted more, but he'd pulled away. And now, he wanted her to think logically?

She blinked several times, processing everything he'd just said and had a question. "Why didn't you just say that a week ago?"

Chase bunched his shoulders. "I wish I had a great answer, but I don't. I'm not perfect, London. I'm going to make mistakes as we navigate our way through this. Hell, the last time I seriously dated, it was the nineties. Are you willing to give me another chance?"

Deep down, London wanted to say yes, but after the

heartache of the last week she needed to be a bit more cautious this time around. "You've given me a lot to think about, Chase." London rose to her feet and reached for her purse. "I'm not saying no, but I need some time to think about this and what I really want."

He nodded.

"Fair enough." He stood to his full six foot three inches of height, dwarfing London. "Can I still call you?"

"Yes," London said. "I'd like that."

A broad grin spread across his full lips. "Then count on it."

After walking London back to her car at Fresh Market, Chase sighed. He'd really made a mess of things with her. That hadn't been his intention. When he'd talked to Mason the previous Saturday, he'd felt hopeful, ready to tackle the world and give a relationship with London a try. Then later that night he'd suffered another nightmare. This one more devastating and traumatizing than the night before with London.

It had set him back. He'd woken up the next day, irritable and distant. That feeling had lingered in him for the rest of the day and no one was immune to its impact. At work on Monday, even Mason had given him a wide berth after he'd nearly ripped his head off on the job site.

Chase knew he had to deal with his demons soon. There was no way he could go on like this. But once he was in the middle of an episode, the nightmares came more frequently. It's why he'd begun to doubt whether getting involved with London was wise. And so one day had moved into the next and next, until he was standing in front of London at Fresh Market feeling like a heel.

He'd never wanted to make her feel cheap or used, but that's exactly what he'd done. He had to get through to her and if that meant being real and more honest than he'd ever been with a woman, then so be it. He'd let it all out, put it all on the line. Tell her his greatest fears. He just hoped that London would agree to continue to see him and that she wouldn't be one of his greatest regrets.

The next week, London was surprised at the large amount of time and effort Chase was putting into making her feel special. Admittedly, she was suspicious, but Chase called her when he said he would. In fact, he called her during his lunch and both breaks on the construction job he was working on, but the calls were usually preceded by a morning text that reminded London he was thinking of her or wishing her a great day.

Due to his persistence, London wanted to give him a second chance and did just that during a call the following week. Chase seemed surprise at first, but then she could hear the elation in his voice over the fact that she was willing to see him again. Then he quickly asked her out on their second date.

His choice of venue surprised her big time, however.

"You want me to go with you to your friend's for dinner?" It was an odd choice for a second date. She'd thought he would want them to spend some alone time.

"Yes, I do. I want you to get to know them. Mason is my oldest friend. We met when we were both stationed in Germany."

"Then I would love to go with you," London said.

She liked that Chase wanted her to meet his friends. She knew she shouldn't compare him to Shawn, but Shawn hadn't been eager for her to meet his buddies. He'd tried to keep that meeting from happening until they had dated nearly a year. London had begun to feel like his dirty little secret, like he didn't want anyone to know he was seeing a plus-sized girl. Eventually he'd relented, but not after a lot of whining on her part.

As for Chase, she loved that he was trying to show her that he wanted to get to know her on a deeper level by including her in his life. It meant a lot.

"Good, I'll arrange for Saturday night and pick you up," Chase responded.

And just like that, Chase was starting to redeem himself in London's eyes.

Chapter 10

"I HATE COMING HERE," CHASE TOLD Dr. Burke, the therapist Mason had recommended. This was Chase's second visit to the doctor's home office in the Garden district.

Chase hadn't exactly been anxious to have his head shrunk again and have someone throw psychobabble at him. But he also wasn't proud of how he'd treated London just because she'd gotten close and seen him at his lowest. And because he'd been afraid of the feelings she'd evoked, he'd shut her out. He was lucky that London was a forgiving person and willing to give him another chance after he'd basically hit it and quit it.

Although that was his usual MO, meeting London had made him want to change that and delve deeper beyond the surface than in his previous relationship incarnations.

And so he'd gotten the therapist info from Mason and contacted him more than a week ago. Dr. Burke had told him they'd focus on exposure therapy again as he'd encountered in the military. They would focus on memories that were less upsetting for Chase before talking about worse ones so he would get desensitized, so eventually he could deal with bad memories a little bit at a time.

And so here he was on a shrink's couch.

"I can see that you don't want to be here. You seem uncomfortable, Chase," Dr. Burke said. "You don't have to lie on the sofa you know. You can sit up and talk to me like you would anyone else."

"Is that right?"

The doctor nodded. "I want you to feel like this is a safe and secure refuge for you."

"One day a week?" Chase snorted.

"You can come more if you like."

"I'd much rather have teeth pulled with no anesthesia."

The doctor chuckled. "You don't believe in therapy, I take it?"

"One shrink session a week will do little to heal the scars I have, Doc."

"Why don't you tell me about those scars?"

Chase laughed bitterly. "Just jump right into the deep end, huh?"

"Or wherever you feel most comfortable."

Chase rose to his feet and began pacing the room. "Don't you get it? None of this is comfortable or normal. It's not normal to have a recurring nightmare for years on end. It's not normal to see the faces of the men you've lost in your dreams."

"It is if you're suffering from PTSD," Dr. Burke replied, "but I think you already know that. According to the chart you brought me, you were diagnosed before you left the military. Looks like you underwent some exposure therapy a few years ago."

"Yeah," Chase said, "what of it?"

"How did you feel about talking about your trauma repeatedly? Did you ever feel like you were learning to get control of your thoughts and feelings about the trauma so that you wouldn't be afraid of your memories any longer?"

"No," Chase stated bluntly.

"Is that why you never continued therapy?"

"It wasn't going to bring my dead friends back to life," Chase responded, walking back to the couch and sitting down. "And watching *Lion King* as therapy to let go some of my anger sure as hell didn't, though I have to admit I really dig Scar."

"You identify with Scar?" Dr. Burke scribbled notes on his notepad. "Why is that?"

"Really, Doc? We're going to analyze my interpretation of the *Lion King*?"

"Do you identify with Scar because he's damaged? Is that how you see yourself? As damaged goods? Unredeemable? Unlovable?"

"Wait a sec," Chase's voice rose. "I never said I was unlovable."

"But isn't that how you felt when your ex-wife Bianca cheated on you?"

Chase frowned. "That didn't make me unlovable. It made me stupid for not seeing the signs sooner, for not realizing that the bitch was going behind my back and sleeping with who I thought was my best friend."

"She betrayed you. Like Scar betrays his brother. Do you want revenge?"

"I got that," Chase responded. "I left her penniless, but she'd already found another luckless soldier. There's women like that, you know, who prey on military men in the hopes we might die or be blown up in the desert."

"That's a blanket statement."

"But true," Chase said.

"Have you shared this cynical view of women with London, the new woman you're seeing?"

Chase smiled at hearing London's name. "Of course not. Because from what I can see, London's nothing like Bianca. She's good and kind, a decent person. She would never betray someone because she knows what that feels like."

"Why is that?"

"Because her husband cheated on her too."

"Two kindred spirits," Dr. Burke replied.

"Something like that."

"London's the real reason you're here."

"No, not entirely. I want the nightmares to end so I can spend the night with my woman and not be afraid I'm going to attack her in the middle of the night."

"But you have to be willing to put in the time, Chase, or this is never going to work."

Chase sighed. "I'm here, aren't I? So let's talk."

London was excited to have a night to herself. She was taking some much needed ME time. She would see Chase on Saturday night, when she would have dinner with him at his friend Mason's. All she wanted right now was to curl up with a good book on her couch and drink a glass of wine.

Unfortunately, her sister Bree had called her several times over the last week. She wanted to avoid Bree, so she'd ignored the calls. She knew that her sisters wanted to come for a visit to New Orleans in an effort to bond.

London knew her sisters genuinely cared about her well-being and wanted to bridge the gap between them since they hadn't grown up together, but she wasn't sure she could do it. She made the obligatory phone calls and sent the occasional texts to catch up on what was going on in their lives; but they weren't her first call if something went down. Violet was. She was more of a sister than Jada and Bree had ever been.

But they were making an effort, so London supposed she should too.

After pouring herself a glass of wine in the kitchen, London went in search of her smartphone. She found it lying on the cocktail table. Tucking her feet underneath her, London hit the speed dial.

Bree answered on the third ring. "London, it's so good to finally hear from you. You're awfully hard to reach these days."

"I'm sorry about that," London apologized. "I've just been really busy with work and..." Her voice trailed off.

She could hear curiosity in Bree's voice. "And what? What aren't you telling me?"

"Nothing serious," London replied, "or at least not yet." She sighed. "I'm sort of seeing someone."

"Sort of?" Bree chuckled. "Does he know about it?"

London let out a hearty laugh. "Of course. It's just that our relationship is still very new so I'm not ready to qualify it yet."

"I can understand that. Will Jada and I get the chance to meet him when we come to visit you?"

London was silent for several moments. She wasn't sure she was ready to share Chase with the world. On the other hand, he had met her grandparents. "Sure," she finally responded. "It'll be fun."

"I'm so excited to meet him," Bree said, "and to spend some quality time with you. You can show us around the Big Easy."

"You've never been?"

"I came for a work trip once, but I'm afraid I didn't have any time for sightseeing."

That was her sister Bree. She was all work and no play. London wondered if she ever made time to have a social life. She supposed she would find out during their visit. "Then that means I'll have to show you my city, because New York isn't the only city that never sleeps. Wait until you experience Bourbon Street. It's an experience like no other."

"I can't wait to taste your food at Shay's," Bree commented. "Daddy says it's all the rage."

"Is that right?" London had to admit she was surprised their father was giving her praise for her culinary skills because he certainly hadn't been thrilled with her choice of profession. Said he'd never wanted her to have to work so hard, but London didn't mind hard work and a little sweat and tears. It's what made her who she was.

"Daddy says you're *the* best chef in N'awlins," Bree dragged out the name.

London laughed to herself. "And he's just a little bit biased."

"He loves you, you know," Bree replied. "I know you've always had a beef with him, but you're the oldest, London. And just as important to him as Jada and I. And of course, Trent."

London rolled her eyes at the addition of their half-brother Trent as an afterthought. He would always be the black sheep of the family. "Thank you for saying that."

"But you don't think I mean it?" Bree sounded miffed.

"It's not that. Listen, Bree, you just don't understand what it's like being in my shoes. I didn't grow up with the illustrious Duke Hart as my father."

"And you hate that we did?" Bree observed. "But I can't change the past or give you back the years you missed with our father. All I can do is try and bridge the gap between us. I thought or I hoped you were on board with that."

London sighed with exasperation. "I am," she stated. "I'm sorry if I gave you the impression that I'm not."

"Are you sure," Bree pressed, "because if you'd rather Jada and I not come, we'll stay away."

"No, no, no," London spoke quickly. "Please come. I'm sorry if I was testy. My relationship with Duke is our fight, not yours. And I would like to try to bridge the gap as well, but you have to understand it won't happen overnight. We've got years to make up for."

"Agreed," Bree said. "But I'm willing to try if you are."

"I am."

"Well good, because Jada and I will be there in a few weeks."

"You sure don't waste any time do you?" London replied.

"Never have, never will."

Bree's personality was no-nonsense and London liked that about her because she had a low-BS tolerance after Shawn. "See you soon."

Chase picked London up from her house on Saturday night and drove her to Mason's place. London was pleasantly surprised that Chase was opening his life up to her. It told her that this time around he wanted to give their relationship a legitimate shot at flourishing.

However, she was a little nervous to meet Chase's friends and hoped they'd like her. After Chase had told her that Mason's wife, Kelly, was a homemaker and would most likely cook a down-home meal, London decided she'd dress up for the date. So tonight she wore white wide-legged linen pants and a black shell with a white moto jacket over it. She paired the ensemble with a simple dangling silver necklace and black wedges.

Chase commented on how sophisticated she looked as he opened his passenger door for her.

"Did I overdress?" London asked when she hopped out of his truck in front of Mason's bungalow-style house.

Chase glanced down at his jeans and button-down shirt. "Babe, you look good in anything. I think I'm underdressed."

"You look great." London reached inside the truck to pull out the bottle of Cabernet Sauvignon and flowers she'd brought for their hosts.

Chase took the gifts out of her hands and led her up the concrete driveway to the front door, all the while keeping his hand on the small of her back.

"You ready?" Chase asked just as the front door opened.

An enormous fella who looked like he could be a linebacker for the New Orleans Saints charged at them. He enveloped Chase in a bear hug and lifted all six foot three of him off the ground. London was afraid what he would do to her—probably crush her and she was no wallflower.

She was impressed by the man's height—add to that his piercing blue eyes, and London was sure he'd left some broken hearts behind when he'd married.

Eventually the two men separated and Chase turned to her. "Mason, I'd like to introduce you to London Hart. London, this is my boy, Mason Dillard. We go w-a-a-a-y back."

London gave Mason a warm smile and offered him her hand. "Great to meet you." But instead of taking her hand, Mason treated her to the same bear hug he'd bestowed on Chase. London could barely breathe. Chase tapped his arm.

"Mason, ease up. She can't breathe." Chase pulled Mason off her. When he did, London took a step back to catch her breath.

"Sorry." Mason grinned sheepishly. "It's great to meet you, London. C'mon in." He opened the door and motioned for them to enter.

London liked Mason's home immediately and his wife, Kelly, even more. When the threesome arrived to the kitchen, Kelly, a slender blonde with a bright smile, greeted London with the same friendliness as her husband had. London felt at ease.

The house was inviting and felt lived in. In the family room, magazines were strewn across the cocktail table, the sectional looked worn and lived in, and there were several toys scattered on the floor as their five-year-old and three-year-old boys played with toy trucks.

"These are for you, Kelly." Chase handed the flowers to Mason's wife while Mason took the bottle of wine and proceeded to uncork it.

"Mason," Kelly said, sighing, "I'm sure that was supposed to accompany dinner."

Mason turned to Chase and London. "You mind if we open it now?" Chase turned to London, who shrugged. "Well then, we'll open it now," Mason said, and he continued opening the bottle.

"Anything I can do?" London asked, leaving the boys at the bar and joining Kelly at the stove. Kelly was stirring something that smelled delicious.

"Not really," Kelly replied. "I have it all under control." Then she lowered her voice to a low whisper. "But you can tell me about you and Chase."

Chase watched London from across the room while he and Mason drank a beer. The ladies seemed intent on some quiet time together, so after Mason poured each of them a glass of wine, he and Mason had retired to the family room.

London was beautiful and she didn't even know it. There was something about her that stirred something in him that pushed him beyond the boundaries of his comfort level. Before, it had been about physical pleasure, but with London it was more than the powerful pull of his desire. She was never far from his mind.

"You're sprung," Mason said.

"What did you say?" Chase glanced up and looked in his direction.

"I said you've got it bad," Mason replied. "You can't take your eyes off her."

"And that's a problem?"

Mason shrugged. "There's no problem. I've just never seen you like this. This *invested*. You know I'm right, dude. Normally you don't stay long enough to find out anything about your bed bunnies, but it's clear London is different."

"You could say that again," Chase replied. "I can't seem to get her off my mind, not even at work."

Mason inclined his head toward the kitchen and Chase caught London giving him a wink. "Looks like she feels the same way."

"I hope so. I almost blew it because of those damn nightmares, but I'm in therapy now."

Mason tipped his beer bottle back and took a swig. "And how's that going?"

"You know I don't like to be shrinked."

"I didn't know that was a verb," Mason said with a grin.

"It's going," Chase replied.

"And the nightmares?"

"Haven't had any in more than a week," Chase replied, "and don't say it's because of the therapy"—he pointed his index finger at Mason—"because they're known to go away, but when they return, they come roaring back."

"The therapy will help keep them at bay."

"Why are you such a proponent of talking things out?" Chase asked. If it was up to him, he'd prefer to keep his feelings to himself. Before he passed, his father had taught him that real men never cried. And he never had. Not at his father's funeral or at the funerals of the fallen men in his unit.

"Dinner's ready," Kelly called over to them from the kitchen.

"Talking things out gets it off your chest," Mason said. "You'll be amazed at how relieved you'll feel. Coming, honey."

Chase thought about Mason's musings as he joined London, Kelly, and Mason at the eat-in table in the kitchen. London was sitting across from him, which would allow him to play footsy with her.

Kelly had laid the table out informally with the casserole dishes in the center. "Help yourself," she said, "we don't stand on ceremony here." She got her two boys situated in their high-chairs, then set heaping bowls of macaroni and cheese in front of them. Then Kelly adjusted her shift dress and took a seat at the table.

London was the first to indulge in the first casserole dish before passing it around. Chase followed her lead and tried a little bit of everything until there wasn't any empty room in sight on his plate. "Looks good, Kel."

She beamed. "Why thank you. I do try to be a good wife and have a meal waiting for Mason while he's out there supporting this family."

"So you're a stay-at-home mom?" London asked.

Kelly nodded. "Never thought I would be. I'd always been a career woman and after Benji"—she turned to her oldest son, Benjamin, and ruffled his hair—"I tried to do it all, juggling work and family, but after Nolan, it was impossible to ignore the fact that I had two small children who needed their mommy."

London nodded. "I understand. I've always thought that if I ever have children I would love to stay at home, bake cookies, go to the PTA, and be a soccer mom, you know."

"And do you want children?" Kelly inquired, glancing in Chase's direction as she asked the question.

How had Chase gotten on the hot seat? He and London were nowhere near the stage of talking about marriage and babies, but here they were.

London nodded. "Yes, I would." She sipped on her wine. "Someday," she added, glancing hesitantly at Chase.

Luckily his boy saved the day. "Children are a blessing," Mason said, "but they can also be a handful."

And just then, Nolan tossed his drink aside, spilling the contents all over the kitchen floor.

"See what I'm saying?" Mason said as Kelly jumped to her feet and rushed to the sink to grab a dish towel.

The rest of the conversation turned to less controversial topics like sports, movies, and the upcoming mayoral election—and Chase breathed a sigh of relief. He and London hadn't talked about their expectations or hopes for their relationship, but he was sure that conversation would be coming soon since Kelly had put the thought in London's head. In the meantime, London was extremely comfortable hanging around his best friend and wife.

Mason meant a lot to Chase, so it was important that she fit in.

And she did.

London was the type of woman that, if he was ready, he could get serious about.

Hours later, they said their goodbyes to the Dillards and settled back in Chase's truck for the ride back to his place.

"I enjoyed your friends," London commented.

Chase grinned. "I'm glad. I could tell they liked you a lot because they didn't want us to leave."

"That's true." London laughed. "I'm sure Kelly was happy to have adult company since she's stuck in the house with two small children with whom she can't have an intelligent conversation."

Chase threw his head back and let out an uproarious laugh. "You have a point there."

Due to the hour, traffic was light and it didn't take Chase long to make it back to London's. When he did, he let the engine idle and they sat quietly for several moments. Eventually, London spoke. "Wo-would you like to come in—for a drink?"

Chase gripped the steering wheel as he pondered her request. He would love to come in and not just in her house, but he'd made a vow to himself that he would show London the respect she deserved by treating her like the queen she was. When the time was right, they would rekindle their sexual relationship. For now, he'd have to be content with a cold shower despite the protest of the arousal in his jeans. Whenever he was around London, he had a damn near permanent hard-on.

"London." He turned to her and was about to say more, but instead, he lightly stroked her cheek. "Another time?"

"Sure." She reached for the handle on the passenger door, but he reached across and stopped her.

"Don't leave upset. I enjoyed tonight and you getting to

know my friends, but I'm also trying to do the upstanding thing. Be the man you deserve."

"Chase," she said his name so softly, "you're already that man. I don't expect you to be anyone except yourself, because that's the man I'm *feeling.*"

"Oh yeah? You care to show me?"

"I would," London replied, "but since you've turned down my request to come in, I guess this will have to do." She leaned over across the gearstick and kissed him. At first the kiss was soft and sweet, but something ignited in Chase.

London was lighting a fire in him that had to be fed. On the second kiss, his mouth crashed down on hers as he gave into the hunger. She kissed him back with an equal frenzy of passion, and her hands tangled around his neck drawing him closer. Their tongues dueled, teeth scraped, their lips molding and meshing together as the need to taste each other became second only to breathing.

If Chase could have, he would have pulled London across the gearshift, put her on his lap and make her ride him until they both came hard and fast. Instead his hands were entwined in her hair, tugging her forward, so he could shift position and delve his tongue even deeper into her mouth.

"Chase," she groaned out his name when he began to rain kisses on her eyelids, cheeks, and then back to her mouth.

Chase knew he had to pull back. If he didn't, he would take her up on her request. Slowly, he released her and leaned back in his driver's seat, taking in deep gulps of air.

He glanced sideways at London and she was equally as ravaged. Hopping out of the truck, he came over to the passenger side. "C'mon, let me walk you inside."

The lust in her eyes as she looked into his almost made Chase regret his conviction, but in the end he stood his ground. He deposited her safely at her front door and after planting a chaste kiss on her forehead, he drove off.

Chase wasn't sure just how long he could be the good guy because with a woman as passionate as London, it was just a matter of time before the inevitability of ending up back in bed occurred. And for Chase, that wouldn't be soon enough.

Chapter 11

C HASE CONTINUED TO TURN UP the romance dial. If he wasn't phoning or texting, he and London were spending valuable time together and not in the bedroom. He seemed determined to prove to her that sex wasn't the only reason he wanted to get to know her. He actually cared and wanted to know the person inside—though London's libido wished they'd share another night like that first passionate encounter at his apartment.

London had never felt that instant spark with another man before like she felt with Chase. With Shawn, he'd been more like a crush. She'd been willing to do anything for him because she hadn't believed a man as fine as Shawn would be interested in a big girl like her. She'd always been self-conscious about her plus-size figure and marrying Shawn and his subsequent betrayal of their marriage had done little to boost her self-confidence.

Chase, on the other hand, was exactly *what* and *who* she needed to boost it. He luxuriated in her curves and never put her down or made her feel bad about her size. In fact, if she didn't eat or attempted to push her food around on the plate as she'd done so many times with Shawn, Chase would encourage her to enjoy her food instead.

They were having one of those nights that evening, a week after their date at Mason's place. Chase had picked her up at her apartment after she'd worked a portion of the dinner rush and then rushed home to change.

She'd put on her favorite pair of fitted jeans and an off – the-shoulder peasant top with chandelier earrings and high-heeled sandals. Chase had given her his sign of approval with a wolfish smile.

Now they'd just finished dinner and were looking at the dessert menu at a romantic French bistro in the French Quarter. She was sure the dinner was costing a mint and shook her head.

"I don't need anything."

"Need?" Chase raised a brow. "Or want? Because the London I know loves dessert."

London blushed. She'd always tried to cover up her love of all things sweet, but Chase loved to indulge her.

"How about this mocha pots de crème?" Chase asked. "It sounds delicious. We can share."

"Well... alright," she finally acquiesced.

Chase looked up at the waitress who was standing near their table. "You heard the lady, we'll have the crème pot."

"I'll get that right out for you."

"Thank you." Chase turned back around and reached for London's hands across the table. "Baby, you can have whatever you want. You don't have to withstand on my account. I've got this."

London bunched her shoulders. "I know, but we've been going out to dinner quite a bit and I know how expensive that can get."

"Listen"—Chase lifted his hand and his thumb grazed her chin—"if I couldn't afford it, I wouldn't ask you out. And besides, we ate in the other night at your place and had movie night."

London thought back to several nights ago when they'd cuddled on her couch, watched an action movie on Netflix, and ate microwave popcorn. It had been sheer bliss if only

Chase hadn't eventually disengaged from their tangled limbs to go back to his place, leaving her feeling lusty.

"True," London replied. "I did enjoy staying in on the couch."

"And I love showing my lady a good time."

"And is that what I am?" London inquired. They hadn't exactly given their relationship a title yet, much less talked about where it was going, but she felt like his woman.

"Yes, you are," Chase stated unequivocally.

"I like the sound of that."

"Then give me some." Chase leaned across the table and brushed his lips across hers. When their lips touched, sparks of hunger shot through London, but just as quick as the sparks flamed, he pulled away and sat back in his seat.

The waitress brought the decadent pudding dessert to their table along with two spoons and they indulged in its gooey deliciousness. After washing it down with a cappuccino, they ended the evening with a stroll through the French Quarter. London didn't want the night to end because then she'd have to go back home alone and take a cold shower.

Chase must have felt the same way because they continued walking until they hit the music district. The strains of blues and jazz could be heard from the storefronts of several establishments.

Chase looked at her. "I know you have to be at Shay's in the morning for Sunday brunch, but what do you say we check out one of these blues clubs?"

London smiled. "Would love it."

They continued for another few yards until they hit a spot playing some old school blues. The place was packed and there wasn't an empty table in sight. Strings of twinkle lights hung from the rafters and images of famous blues singers like Ray Charles, Etta James, BB King, and Muddy Waters lined the walls along with posters of upcoming events around New Orleans. The lead singer of the band was singing a mid-temp song that had the drummer, guitarist, and saxophonist firing up the crowd.

Chase squeezed through the audience until he reached the wooden bar and staked his claim. He moved London until she stood in front of him. Then he wrapped his arms around her and pulled her closer, allowing her to use his body as a post to lean against.

It felt good to be in close contact with him and London wanted more, but instead Chase whispered, "Would you like a drink?"

"Yeah, I'd like that."

And so she had a whiskey to ease the tension she felt at being near Chase, especially him acting like a boy scout. A second and a third soon followed, which she pretty much guzzled after the first. The liquor was like fire going through her veins, but London didn't care. She needed something to ease the ache she felt inside.

"Easy, love." Chase took the drink from her hand and placed it on the bar. "Whiskey is meant to be sipped."

"I know that," London said coyly with a languid smile. She was starting to feel the effects of drinking the three drinks so rapidly.

Eventually the lead singer slowed the pace to a raspy blues song that had a handful of couples taking to the floor and swaying to the music. Chase and London weren't far behind. Soon, London was encased in his strong arms, but that isn't what got her blood boiling. It was when he slid his leg between her thighs and began swaying her dirty dancing style to the music.

Feeling Chase's muscular thigh between her quivering ones sent London into overdrive and she shamelessly rubbed herself against him, desperate for the friction. She heard Chase's low guttural groan as she rubbed her clit against him.

"Jesus, London," Chase whispered in her ear, "do you have any idea what you're doing to me?"

"I could do a whole lot more," she stated boldly. She glanced up to see that Chase's eyes had become dark and stormy.

Or should she say hot with desire for her?

"C'mon, let's get out of here." He shifted upright and slowly got them both off the small dance floor.

Once they were outside, Chase took her hand and led her down the crowded street. For a Saturday night, there were still plenty of revelers enjoying the music district and Bourbon Street. When they made it to Chase's F-150, he opened the passenger side. "Get in."

Despite her height, London stumbled as she got up into the high vehicle. Chase lifted her tush and she tumbled inside very unladylike. She righted herself just as he got in on the driver's side.

He glanced in her direction as he started the engine. "You're drunk."

"Am not."

"Are too," he said with a smile and quickly pulled out into the road. "Why don't you lie back, beautiful, and I'll wake you when we reach your place."

"I'm not sleepy," London replied, "I'm horny."

A broad smile spread across Chase's face as he glanced in her direction. "Oh yeah?"

"Yes. So what are you going to do about it?"

"I guess you'll have to wait and see."

Chase parked his truck in front of London's home and turned off the engine. Glancing over at his passenger, he saw that she was sound asleep, her head resting against the door. His gaze traveled over her face, then moved over her body slowly.

He was trying to do right by her. Show her he wasn't

just about sexing her up, but she was making it damn hard when she said things like she was horny and what was he going to do about it. He'd like nothing better than to show her just how turned on he'd been in at the blues club. Having her rub her hot, heated flesh against his groin had made him swell to life. He'd had to mentally will his growing member to stand down.

But his erection was just as hard now as it was then.

London was in no condition to consent to the kind of back-breaking sex he had in mind, though. He suspected that her drinking heavily tonight was a way to take the edge off. And he understood. Since he was determined to woo London and show her he was a good man and not like the knucklehead of an ex-husband she'd had, he'd taken to going to the gym to cool down his libido. He'd run a punishing five miles and spar with any man brave enough to take him on there.

And it had worked.

Until tonight.

London had tested his resolve. Made him want to break all the rules he'd set for himself, for their relationship. He jumped out of the truck and came around to her side. Opening the door, London stirred and stared at him sleepily as he unbuckled her seatbelt.

"C'mon, baby." He helped her out of the passenger seat.

She stumbled again, but he had a grip on her and held her firmly upright as he helped her up the steps to her house.

"Am I drunk?" she asked, laughing up at him.

"Oh yes, baby, you're most definitely drunk." He reached for her purse and fished her house keys out, opening the front door.

Once they were inside, he tossed her purse and keys down and walked her to her bedroom. When they made it to the bed, London spun around to face him and without missing a beat began to unbutton her shirt. "Then that

132

means you can take advantage of me," she said with a wicked smile. She released several more buttons allowing Chase to see the lace bra she wore underneath.

He groaned.

"The only thing I'm going to do," he said, lightly pushing her backward to sit down on the bed so he could take off her shoes, "is help you get to bed *alone*." He emphasized that last word.

She frowned. "That's no fun."

Once the other shoe was off, he pulled back the comforters and motioned for her to get inside. "Aren't you going to undress me?" London asked playfully.

Chase's eyes zeroed to where the swell of her luscious cleavage beckoned to him, thanks to the buttons London had undone. He'd love nothing better than to strip her naked and suck on those delicious breasts of hers all night long while he was buried deep inside her, but he'd never taken advantage of an intoxicated woman. And he wasn't about to start now.

Chase grasped the coverlet and eased it over London's figure. He stroked her cheek with his palm. "Another time."

"Can't you at least stay with me?" London inquired. "We don't have to *do* anything."

"I don't know, London. I don't think that's a good idea."

"Please?"

He would regret it later, but Chase agreed to sleep with London. Or at least next to her, but he stayed on top of the coverlet instead of inside its warmth where London was cocooned. Her pleas had quieted when he'd wrapped his arms around her midriff and eventually, she'd drifted off to sleep. As did Chase.

Boom. Boom
The sound of gunfire and grenades erupted through the

village as Chase and his men went into combat. It was his job to ensure the perimeter of the village was safe, but he and his men were catching enemy fire from every angle. There were men on the ground and men on the roof with guns all aimed at them.

Chase knew if he didn't make a move soon, they would be surrounded with no way out. He gave the signal for the men to move forward in wedge position and together he and his platoon pushed forward. They'd nearly made it to the other end of the village when a tanker sprang up from a trench and came barreling toward them. A man was in the turret pointing a machine gun at them.

There was no way out.

And no place to hide.

There would be casualties and loss of life. Chase just didn't know how many.

As the sound of the gunfire rang out a hundred yards in front of him, Chase watched in horror as several of his men dropped to their knees and keeled over.

"Noooo!" Chase raced toward them, waving his hands to warn them, but it was too late.

Chase bolted upright in the bed.

"Chase?" He heard London's voice in the fog of his brain and turned to find her sitting beside him on the bed, holding a glass of water. "Are you okay?"

Instead of answering her, he reached for the glass and chugged the water down his parched throat. He handed it back to her and flipped his legs over the side of the bed.

"Chase, where are you going?"

"Home," he said, bending down next to the bed to tie his shoes.

"You don't have to go because you had a nightmare," London stated. "You could stay here with me. Let me help you."

Help him? Hell, he wasn't sure if that was even

possible. Wasn't therapy supposed to help rid him of the nightmares? And they had to a degree, but in the back of his mind, the horrors and atrocities that he'd seen or done still lived on in his mind.

Chase shook his head. "It's best if I go, sweetheart." When he was finished tying his shoes, he rose to his full height and headed for the door, but London blocked it.

"Please don't leave like this," she pleaded. "The last time you had a nightmare I didn't see or hear from you for a week."

Chase hated to hear the stone-cold facts, but London was right. He'd retreated into himself because he hadn't wanted her to see him like this. And he still didn't. The only difference was that this time he wouldn't run away or turn his back on her.

"I promised you, London, that things would be different," Chase responded softly, stroking her cheek. "And they will be. I won't abandon you like before."

He saw the doubt creep into her brown eyes and knew he'd put it there. His own insecurity about his PTSD had made London fearful that the first time things got rough, he'd get going.

"I promise, baby." He pulled her into his arms. At first, he felt her resistance, so he lowered his head and captured her soft lips in a kiss while his hands roamed over her backside. He cupped her firmly against his middle.

He could feel her begin to squirm. Encouraged, he deepened the kiss. He loved how she tasted and how their tongues dueled together in perfect harmony. When he finally lifted his head, they were both breathless.

"I will call you later, alright?" Chase said. "I promise."

"C'mon, Doc," Chase said, pacing Dr. Burke's office a few days later. "I thought my coming here was supposed to help. But instead there I was screaming in the middle of the night again and giving London a fright. She didn't think I saw it, but there was fear in her eyes though she would never admit it."

"Have you ever hurt London or any other woman while in the throes of one of your nightmares?"

Chase snapped his fingers. "Stay focused, Doc. I've told you that I've never stuck around in any woman's bed long enough to find out. After we'd done the deed, I was gone and home to my own bed, not terrorizing random women."

"And why do you think that is?"

Chase frowned and stopped pacing long enough to ask, "Why do you ask?"

"I want to know why you've been sleeping with random women who mean nothing to you."

"Because I needed to erase the memory of Bianca, my cheating, faithless ex-wife," Chase returned sharply. "And trust me, I'm not proud of how I behaved with some women. I used them, but they used me to, whether I was a one-night stand or they just needed the affection and comfort of a man."

"But you don't see the need to rid Bianca from your mind anymore. Does that mean you've forgiven her?"

"Hell no," Chase said. "I know I'm not blameless in the failure of our marriage. I was gone for too many tours, but that didn't give her the right to cheat on me. If she wanted out, she should have said so."

"And would you have let her, Chase? Or would the pain of losing her have been as bad as losing your parents?"

"What do my *dead* parents have to do with any of this?" Chase gave the doctor a hostile glare. "I came here for answers, but instead you keep asking me questions."

"I think there's a lot of things that have upset you, Chase, but you internalize them and never let them out. Losing your parents. Losing your soldiers. Losing Bianca. Sometimes a person can only take so much loss."

"I don't want to talk about this anymore." Chase started

136

toward the door. He was done with the session and maybe even this whole damn therapy notion. Perhaps he was better off on his own because therapy sure hadn't helped him when he was in London's bed a few nights ago.

"If you haven't figured it out, Chase, running away won't solve your problems."

"Go to hell!" Chase said on his way out the door.

Chapter 12

L ONDON COULDN'T RECALL A TIME when she'd felt this good about herself. Violet commented on her new outlook on life the next weekend. She and London were out shopping for a new outfit for London's upcoming date with Chase later that evening.

"Someone is feeling awfully chipper these days," Violet remarked as London held up a stunning evening gown against her bosom. She was modeling it in front of a floor-length mirror at their local Macy's.

"And," London said with a smile, "what's wrong with that?"

Chase had kept his word and not only called her but she'd seen him since her drunken episode and his nightmare the previous weekend. She only wished Chase would allow her to help him, but he was very close-mouthed on the subject. And as much as she wanted to be there for him, he would have to come to her when he was ready.

"Absolutely nothing," her friend responded. "Just tell me where I can sign up to find me another Chase and I will happily skip right along with you. I can't believe how much that man has you beaming like a neon sign."

London pulled down the dress and moved closer to the mirror. "I'm not that bad, am I?"

"Uh, yes," Violet said. "You've been talking nonstop about Chase this and Chase that."

"Because he's done a complete 360," London replied. "He's been wooing me with phone calls, texts, and dinners out. And now The Jazz and Heritage Gala."

"Yeah, what's up with that?" Violet asked. "Where does a guy like Chase working a construction job get tickets to a star-studded soiree like that?"

London shrugged. "Don't know and don't care. I've never attended something so swanky." She reached for another dress hanging on the hook. "What about this one?" She held up a simple black hourglass gown.

Violet shook her head. "Boring. Plain. Any one of those adjectives."

London frowned.

"Hey, if you wanted someone to sugarcoat it, you should have asked someone else, but if you want Chase's eyes to pop out of his sockets, then you'll listen to my advice." Violet rose and reached for a beaded V-neck halter floor-length gown. It had a fitted bodice decked out with a dense mix of shimmery beading and sequins that got lighter through the relaxed skirt.

"I don't know," London said. She stared openmouthed at the gown. An ample amount of her bosom would be on display.

"Try it on!" Violet pushed her toward the dressing room.

"Alright, alright." Reluctantly, London went inside one of the rooms. Five minutes later, she emerged in the sexy sequined dress to face the three-way mirror.

London had to admit she liked what she saw and a large grin spread across her face.

"See," Violet said from the couch she was perched on outside the dressing room. "Do I know my stuff or what?"

London turned around to glare at her. "Yes, you do, my dear, and I LOVE it!" She glanced back over her shoulder to look at herself in the mirror. "Oh yes, this is the one."

After she changed back into her street clothes, London

met Violet back on the sales floor so they could shop for shoes to accompany the dress.

"Chase will be salivating all night seeing you in that dress. He'll be ready to ravage you when he gets you back to your place."

"I highly doubt that."

Violet's brow arched. "Why would you say that?"

"He hasn't tried to get me into bed since that first night we slept together. And that's not to say he's lost his swagger and the come-ons have completely gone away. He *has* been romantic and thoughtful, but there's been no action."

Violet laughed. "That's 'cause he knows he screwed up with you at first and any chance of him getting the booty was slim to none."

"That's the thing, Violet," London said as she turned to stare at her friend, "I forgave him, but we've been celibate since our first date."

"C'mon, you've got to be kidding. As hot as you said the sex was?"

"Oh, it was hot," London said, lowering her voice when another patron walked past them to scour the store's clearance rack. "It was the best sex I've ever had, which is why I've been dying for him to make a move, but he hasn't. Why do you think that is?"

"Maybe he thinks he'll be shot down?" Violet answered. "I mean, he did snub you after your one and only night together. He could be a little gun-shy. Have you given him a hint that you're interested in going beyond holding hands?"

London thought about Violet's questions. She certainly knew she wasn't sending him the hands-off vibe. She always made sure to make eye contact or touch him when the moment presented itself. And then there was that drunken night last week when she'd come onto him. "I know I haven't given off the wrong vibe, so what should I do?"

"You're going to have to seriously put the moves on him?"

London frowned. "I dunno, Violet. I'm kind of old school. I prefer an alpha male to take charge."

"And Chase is all that, if somewhat neutered right now, so if you want to refrain from getting cobwebs down below"—Violet motioned downward with her hands—"then I suggest you take matters into your own hands and let the man know you're really feeling him."

London thought about Violet's advice as she surveyed the gown she'd purchased along with a new lingerie set with a matching lace bra and panties. The material would barely cover her ample bosom and overly large bottom. She would wear the ensemble underneath the gown. Maybe if she felt sexy underneath, it would help with her confidence with showing Chase that she wanted to *feel him.*

Chase stared at himself in the mirror as he splashed on some aftershave after a hot shower. He'd gone to the barbershop earlier that morning so his hair could be freshly cut for his date later with London at The Jazz and Heritage Gala.

London had been shocked, to say the least, when he'd told her to pull out her finest duds because he was taking her for a night out on the town and to clear her weekend schedule. Chase wasn't the sort of guy who went to charity galas—he just barely kept his fingernails neat and clean—but thanks to a side job he and Mason had done for one of the big bosses at their construction company, he'd hit the jackpot.

Chase had needed a little extra cash when he'd arrived for his first month's rent and security deposit, so helping Mason out on remodeling the boss's house had been a no-brainer. The guy had thanked them both with VIP tickets that included entry into the exclusive Jazz and Heritage

Gala. The boss had also given Chase VIP tickets to The New Orleans Jazz & Heritage Festival for the next day, which included access to the main stages with a premium viewing area.

As Chase pulled on his tuxedo jacket over his crisp white tuxedo shirt, he felt lucky that he would have London on his arm tonight. He had a lot of demons to exercise and he was trying to do that—and fortunately for him, London was giving him the room to do so. Much to his chagrin, however, he'd listened to Mason's advice and had met with his therapist a few days ago. Chase hadn't exactly been thrilled at laying his heart bare once again to a stranger who couldn't relate to the stress and pain he'd endured during his twenty years in the military. And he'd been right to be wary.

Dr. Burke had never served in the armed forces a day in his life. He was one of those pretty boys who'd gone off to college instead of enduring the tough lessons that the military life taught you. *How can he understand my struggles?* Chase shook his head. And he didn't. Their last session had been a bust and Chase was altogether sure he did not want to go back for a repeat performance.

But tonight, he was determined to put all of that out of his mind for a few hours. He grabbed the corsage out of the fridge he'd gotten for London and headed out to pick up his woman.

Chase was bowled over when London opened the door to her home half an hour later. She was the vision of a golden goddess standing in front of him. Her makeup was flawless and accentuated her full face and slight dimple in her right cheek. Her hair was piled high on her head in a luxurious array of riotous curls and she wore a body-hugging dress that snuggled up against every inch of her voluptuous curves. On top of that, the swell of her ample breasts peeked from the V-neck of her halter dress.

Chase licked his lips. "London, you look stunning," he finally said when the power of speech returned to his brain.

London blushed. "Thank you. I'm glad you like it."

"*Like* is not the word I would use to describe what I'm feeling," Chase replied. The word that came to his mind was *horny* because his erection sprung to life at the sight of her. He'd love nothing better than to slowly peel back every layer of her dress with his mouth, with his tongue. *Jesus!*

"You ready to go?" London asked.

He nodded. "If you are."

"Let me just grab my wrap." London spun on her heel and headed toward her bedroom, giving Chase time to enjoy the view as she walked away.

He would have to get his mind out of the gutter, otherwise it would make for a very long night.

Inwardly, London was thrilled at Chase's response to her new dress. She'd taken great care when dressing that evening. Truth be told, she'd done it for herself, but also for Chase. She wanted him to want her, find her desirable. She ached for him to touch her like he had done the one and only night they'd been intimate.

And she wanted it again.

But could she ask for it?

Show Chase she wanted him to take her to bed and make passionate love to her until her legs turned to jelly? Because that's exactly what she wanted, needed, craved. As excited as she was to go to the gala, London also knew that she would be a tight bundle of nerves at Chase's nearness.

And she was.

When his hand lightly touched her back and helped

her inside the truck, or when he grasped her hand to pull her to the hotel's entrance, or when he tucked her arm between his, London felt giddy. It certainly helped her ignore the shocked glances of the other guests at Chase's choice of vehicle. Most of the vehicles pulling up to the red carpet weren't a big truck, but that was just fine with her. Chase didn't put on any airs. He was who he was—a man's man. And she was proud to be there with him.

As they entered the foyer of the Hilton Riverside, the site of the gala, London thought she wouldn't know anyone there, but surprisingly she knew several people. She introduced Chase to a few city council members that liked to frequent Shay's and a couple of members from her church.

"Would you like a glass of champagne?" Chase whispered in her ear when they finally separated from the group.

"Would love one."

While London stood away from the throng of folks waiting for drinks, she felt the hairs on the back of her neck stand up. She sensed him before she actually saw him.

How could she forget the man who'd singlehandedly caused her to doubt herself? With his tawny skin, sculptured mustache, goatee, and slender build, Shawn Garrett was the man London thought she'd always wanted— an intellectual who just happened to be sexy as hell. She'd been wrong on both accounts. Shawn perpetrated like he was book smart when instead he just knew how to tell you what you wanted to hear. And as for sexy, Chase had more going for him than Shawn ever did.

Turning around slowly, she saw her ex-husband standing a few feet away. Shawn was wearing a white tuxedo with white pants and looked quite dapper. But then she saw his companion, a willowy honey-blonde, and London could feel her blood begin to boil. It was the very blonde who'd been the cause of the demise of their five-year marriage. Shawn noticed her just at that moment, forcing London to plaster a fake smile across her face.

London watched him do a double-take. She was sure he was surprised to see her at a high-society event such as The Jazz and Heritage Gala, but equally so that she was looking just as sophisticated as the hussy he was standing next to.

"London?"

"Don't act dense, Shawn," London told him when he finally reached her. She was nervous and angry, and that made her respond in a rude manner. "We were married for nearly five years after all."

Shawn smiled, revealing pearly-white, very straight teeth. London was sure he'd had dental work because the Shawn she knew had had some jacked-up teeth. She'd always told him to take care of them.

"You're looking well... fed," he responded.

If it weren't for Chase returning with her champagne flute at just that moment, London might have slapped Shawn for the insult. But she needn't have bothered because Chase stepped in.

He wrapped his arm around London's waist and responded with, "I like *my woman* to have a little meat on her bones. I don't really like an anorexic-looking woman, nothing to hold onto, ya know what I mean? But there's no accounting for taste." He handed London her flute.

"Thank you." She took a quick sip of the fizzy drink.

The blonde—Eva was her name—gave Chase an evil glare.

Shawn snorted. "You've certainly found yourself a real man's man there, London." Even at six feet, Shawn had to look up at the skyscraper of a man that was Chase.

"That's right," Chase replied, "so you'd better watch your step."

Shawn's brow rose.

"Chase! There you are," a masculine voice said from behind the group.

Chase and London both turned and saw Mason walking toward them with Kelly. Chase shook his friends' hands and turned to London.

"London, you remember Mason."

London grinned. "Of course, how can I get forget Special Forces. That's my nickname for you," she teased Mason.

"Should I fear for my life?" Shawn snickered from behind them.

London gave her ex-husband the evil eye. As much as she'd love to trade barbs with Shawn, she was happy when Chase placed his hand on the small of her back and led her away from Shawn's vitriol and toward his friends.

"Who is that guy?" Mason asked when they were several feet away from them.

"London's ex," Chase responded, "but I handled him."

Mason grinned. "I just bet you did." He looked at London. "You watch this one," he said, bumping shoulders with Chase, "he's the jealous kind."

"Is that right?" London asked and her eyes connected with Chase's sultry ones. The longing and lust in those dark depths made her forget all about Shawn and vow to focus on herself and Chase for the remainder of the night.

"I can be," Chase whispered, "but you needn't worry."

London wondered if he was thinking of his ex-wife, but she didn't want to think about anyone else but him for the rest of the night.

The doors to the ballroom opened and the hosts began ushering people inside. London released a whoop when she saw that they'd have Harry Connick Jr. as entertainment for the evening. She sure loved her rhythm and blues.

"I'm glad you're excited," Chase whispered from her side, "and that your ex didn't bring down your mood."

"Not tonight," she beamed.

When they found their reserved table, Chase pulled

out her chair and joined her along with Mason and Kelly. Two other couples joined them and made introductions. London was surprised at how comfortable Chase seemed amongst the group. She'd misjudged him thinking he might feel uncomfortable with the high-society crowd, but he conversed with them easily, making light conversation.

Once dinner was served, Chase returned his attention to London and that's where he kept it for the remainder of the evening despite all the speeches and toasts. When the official part of the night was over, the MC announced it was time to party and London and Chase took to the dance floor for the first dance.

Blessedly, the first song was a slow one. London would finally be able to wrap her arms around Chase legitimately and feel his strength. She hadn't known just how much she'd craved a man's touch until Chase had unleashed this passion inside her.

London let out a low moan when Chase pulled her into his embrace and she felt his strong pectorals pressed against her breasts. Her nipples instantly puckered in response to his closeness. And when he lowered his head to rest slightly against hers and placed his hands lightly over her bottom, she was in heaven. She breathed in his unique masculine scent that appealed to everything feminine in her.

"Chase?" London hazarded a glance at him.

"Hmmm?"

"I've missed you," she said. "Missed this."

"Missed what?"

"This closeness," she said quietly against his chest. "This intimacy," she added for effect.

His eyes darkened. "I've missed you too."

"Then wh—" She cut her sentence short. *Am I being too bold?*

"Why have I not made love to you?" he whispered.

She nodded when she saw the naked desire burning in his eyes.

He didn't answer her. Instead he grasped her by the hand and led her off the dance floor and toward the double doors. She didn't even notice that Shawn had been watching their encounter because she was too wrapped up in Chase to see anyone but him.

Chase couldn't believe he'd misread the situation. He'd thought that London would appreciate him being gentlemanly and taking their relationship slow and easy. Instead, he'd made her think that he didn't want her when that was far from the case.

Once they were out of the ballroom and away from prying eyes, Chase pulled London into a secluded corner, grasped both sides of her face, and kissed her.

And it wasn't just any kiss. He'd stored up a lot of passion in the last five weeks as he'd been patiently courting her, but now wasn't that time. He wanted London and pulled her full-figured frame even tighter against his hard chest. When they'd been out there on the dance floor, he'd felt every luscious curve and could feel himself getting aroused.

The look of pure unadulterated lust in her eyes told Chase that rather than *tell* London he wanted her, he needed to *show* her.

And show her he did.

One of his hands spread across the back of her head and his fingers became entwined in her hair. He shifted position so his mouth could crash down on hers with a raw, savage hunger. She kissed him back wantonly, so he pushed his tongue past her full lips to deepen the kiss. She parted them willingly, allowing him to stroke and lick and kiss every inch of her mouth, and then their tongues dueled for more as their lips meshed together to taste everything they could.

Chase felt those chocolate-brown nipples of hers turn into buds against his chest and it caused a stirring in his loins. He grinded the lower half of his body against London and she moaned softly.

That was his undoing. He fitted his mouth over hers, pressing her lips into his. His tongue slid deep, withdrew, slid in again, withdrew. Euphoria spread through him. He'd denied himself, hell the both of them, the pleasure of each other's bodies and he'd had enough. With as much strength as he could muster, he lifted his head and whispered, "Ready to get out of here?"

She responded with an enthusiastic, "Hell yes."

London was achy with need as Chase drove quickly. To her place or his? She didn't know and she didn't care. She just wanted him inside her.

Now.

When Chase had kissed her in that secluded hotel corner, the hot stroke of his skilled tongue had caused heat to pool in the lower half of her body. She'd felt herself becoming slick with desire. Having Chase pressed hard against her, flattening her breasts against him, had made her nipples hard and tight and oh so eager for Chase to give them his undivided attention.

The truck began to slow down and London realized that Chase had brought her back to her place. There was no talking between them and they quickly exited the vehicle and rushed to London's front door. She opened it as quick as she could and Chase followed her inside.

She locked the door behind them and was about to turn around when Chase came behind her and rubbed his erection against her. His hands brushed the hair on her neck aside so he could nuzzle her nape. "See what you do to me?" he muttered roughly. "See how turned on you've got me?"

London felt his arousal and couldn't wait to ride him.

She turned around to face him and without a word began tugging at her dress. As much as she'd loved it, she wanted it off. She wanted to be naked, to feel Chase, skin to skin.

"Here, let me." Chase's hands moved to her back so he could unzip the dress properly. "I've been thinking about doing that all night."

The bodice of the dress fell away to the floor leaving London in her strapless bra and a barely there thong.

Chase licked his lips. "Christ! Had I known you were wearing just that underneath, I would have gotten you out of there much faster."

London beamed. Chase had a way of making her feel like a million bucks without her clothes on. She reached behind her and undid the clasp on her bra. It dropped with a light whoosh to the floor and then she shimmied out of her underwear until she was naked.

"London," Chase began, but he was shocked when she pushed him back against her front door and then kneeled between his legs. Her hands went to his waistband and she opened his slacks before he could protest. She pushed his pants and boxer briefs down to his knees and he helped her by stepping out of them completely. His erection was thick and long between his thighs. London stroked Chase's silky smooth penis with her hands. He was hot and so was she.

Lowering her head, London took him into her mouth. Chase let out a hiss between his teeth. She was sure he hadn't expected her to be so aggressive, but he let her have her way. His hands entwined in her hair, causing pins to fly from her curls, and he squeezed his eyes shut. She tasted him as she felt him throbbing in her mouth. She alternately licked, sucked, and kissed him.

"That's right, London," Chase moaned as she continued to stroke and squeeze him. "That's right, baby, take all of me," he commanded.

She did as instructed, so much so that Chase was coming in her mouth and hurtling swear words as she took him over the edge.

When it was over, she rose to her feet licking away the evidence with her tongue.

"Jesus, London," Chase groaned, "you couldn't wait to let me take you to your bedroom?"

London glanced up to see Chase was still wearing his tuxedo, shirt, socks, and shoes. She smiled wickedly and shook her head. "No. I wanted you so badly, it couldn't wait."

"Well, you know turnabout is fair play."

"I do," London replied, walking backward toward her room, "so why don't you come show me."

Once in her bedroom, Chase quickly began pulling off the rest of his clothes to get naked as fast as possible so he could join her on the bed. The craving to be inside London, to feel her flesh to flesh, man to woman was so intense and his body was demanding satisfaction.

London was splayed across the pillows waiting for him with a seductive come-hither grin and holding a condom.

His eyes glittered as he slithered over to her on the bed. She sheathed him in a matter of seconds and then he pushed her backward to move into position between her legs. He was desperate to answer the urgent yearning that was driving both of them to act out of character and he quickly reached between her legs to ensure she was ready.

And she was.

Hot, wet, and ready for him.

She curled her legs around his hips and he plunged deep inside her as a "Yes" tore from her throat. He felt her inner muscles tighten around him as he bent to kiss her, sweeping his lips over hers. Their mouths wildly matched the thrusting of the lower half of their bodies as Chase rose on both shins and pounded into her.

"Oh God, yes, Chase, yes." London was vocal with her need for him to keep doing exactly what he was doing.

The end result was a fiery explosion that made Chase growl as bliss coursed through his entire body. He collapsed on top of London and then rolled onto his back, carrying her with him. She was splayed across him, one leg entwined between his. They were too limp and relaxed to speak after they'd both had a meltdown.

Chase hadn't known he could feel so intensely possessive and so close to a woman as he felt with London in that moment.

"Happy now?" he asked eventually with a tone of complete satisfaction.

"Mhmm..."

"Glad I could satisfy you."

London lifted her head to glance at him as her fingertips drummed over his chest and his nipples. "There was never any doubt of that."

"Only of my desire for you?" Chase said.

She was silent.

"London," Chase said as he tipped her chin, forcing her to look at him, "I've wanted you, wanted to be with you again after that first night, but considering my behavior afterward, I thought I had to show you that I was worthy of your trust."

She smiled coquettishly. "You've done that. And now... now it's time to make up for lost time."

"And I suppose you have some idea how I can redeem myself?" Chase inquired.

"Oh yes," London replied and reached underneath the covers to find him. His erection swelled back to life. "I have a few in mind."

Chapter 13

C HASE WAS LOOKING FORWARD TO giving London just as much pleasure as she'd just given him. He'd had no idea she was going to go down on him in her foyer. She'd shown him that she desired him as he did her. She'd shown great skill. He'd always prided himself in his prowess in the bedroom and ability to refrain from coming, but London had sucked him off so good, he'd come like a teenage boy.

But now, he intended to remind her she wasn't the only one skilled in the bedroom and she didn't get to take charge anymore. It had been much too long since he'd tasted her and he intended to make up for lost time.

He gripped the one hand she had around him and pulled it up over her head and reached for the other.

"Chase?"

"Shhhh, relax and enjoy."

He slid down her body, lowered his head and spread her legs. Nuzzling in the brown curls at the center of her womanhood, he went in for the kill. He licked, flicked, and teased her with his tongue.

"Chase," she whimpered his name aloud as he darted his tongue in and out of her core.

He lapped at the heat of her sex, stroking her intimately. Her whole body throbbed, but he didn't stop. He was insistent in wanting to feel her body tighten and constrict until she had no choice but to give into its command. And she did. She came around his tongue, screaming out his name until he finally relented.

His erection had lengthened as desire for her coursed through him. He separated from her long enough to put on protection again before retuning back to kiss her. His teeth tugged at her lower lip and then his arm banded around her waist. He kneed her legs apart knowing that she was slick with her juices for him because he'd made her that way. Then he pushed the thick crest of his penis inside her.

London arched against the bed as her body began to accommodate his hard length.

He thrust in again. This time harder. Deeper.

"Take me, baby. Take all of me." Chase's body rocked at the sensation of having London's tight body surround him. He hammered into her long, hard, and thoroughly. His need to have her, possess her was relentless.

She began to come and gasp out his name. "Yes, Chase. Oh God, you feel so good."

He didn't stop. He continued to stroke her, rolling his hips against her. She started coming again. Had she ever stopped?

He pumped inside her until he reached the end of her. Then he roared.

As Chase got out of bed the next morning to make them coffee, London allowed her eyes to enjoy how good he looked without his clothes on. He was all male perfection to her—broad shoulders, a trim waist, muscular legs, and a taut, cheeky behind that she loved squeezing when he was in the midst of hitting her spot.

Last night, she'd felt taken, possessed. Chase was a skillful lover. He knew just where to touch her, lick her, and kiss her to draw out a response from her. His body had pistoned as he slid inside and withdrew, time and time again. He'd used every inch of himself to enslave her and take her to the top of the mountain. His rhythm had been tight and on point until a tidal wave had finally overtaken her.

Honestly, London had lost track of how many times she'd come and eventually she'd drifted off into a deep, unencumbered sleep. And so had Chase. He hadn't had another nightmare beside her and this morning she'd found his backside snuggled against her.

Chase returned to the bedroom several minutes later, unashamed of his nakedness as he carried two steaming mugs of coffee.

"Thank you." London accepted the mug as Chase joined her underneath the covers.

"I hope it's not too strong. After twenty years in the military, it's kind of the only way I drink it."

London smiled. "You're fine. I'm from New Orleans. We like our chicory coffee and it's just as strong as this." She held up her mug.

"So are you ready for the next part of your surprise?"

"What's that?"

He produced tickets from the nightstand drawer. "I have VIP tickets to The New Orleans Jazz & Heritage Festival concert today."

"Get out!"

"It was all part of the ticket package the owner gave Mason and me."

London beamed. "Oh, Chase, this is wonderful, but I've never taken two days off from Shay's."

"I'm sure it'll survive one more day without you. You have to go."

London really wanted to go. And in the end, she did just that. She called her line cook Charlotte and begged her to fill in another day for her. Being the romantic that she was, Charlotte agreed.

Ending the call, London turned to Chase. "I'm all yours."

Chase was pleased with himself. The day with London was going great. They had "Big Chief Experience" VIP tickets, which meant they were enjoying the jazz and heritage festival in top-of-the-line style. They had concert seats in an up-close, exclusive viewing area that was covered from the eighty-degree heat outside.

But that wasn't the best part. They each received ten-minute massages in the Big Chief hospitality lounge along with complimentary champagne and snacks.

"This is wonderful," London gushed, making Chase feel on top of the world for having taken her to this coveted event.

After they had their fill of music, the couple meandered through the Grandstand to look at the vibrant exhibits showing the culture, cuisine, and art that was all things Louisiana. Then it was on to the Folk Village to see the Mardi Gras floats and watch the blacksmiths forge ironwork and musicians handcraft accordions. They ended with the African marketplace, where Chase bought London an irresistible piece of jewelry she'd been eyeing and where she'd returned the favor by purchasing an African sculpture he'd admired.

Chase had never realized just how much culture there was to Louisiana until experiencing it that day with London. Along the way, they stopped and nibbled on pralines, shrimp po-boys, and gumbo from several street vendors.

By the time they made it back to London's later that evening, they were both exhausted, but not enough to keep their hands off each other. Sticky from the hot and humid weather, they'd stripped and stepped into London's walk-in shower. They proceeded to soap and wash each other. Of course for Chase, there wasn't a whole lot of washing going on. Instead, he was touching, molding, and then kissing and licking until eventually he had London backed up against the tile wall with her legs straddled around him as he thrust inside her.

"Put me down," London had pleaded. "You can't hold me up. You'll break your back."

"I'm a lot stronger than you think," Chase had growled and continued pounding into her until she'd eventually let go and given into him.

London had undulated against him and the sweet friction of their slick, wet bodies brought them both to an orgasm much quicker than Chase would have liked. But he would make up for it later. For now, he gave a loud shout as London convulsed around him.

Eventually, when their hunger was sated, they cuddled in bed with Chase's arms wrapped securely around her. "So what's on tap for next weekend?" Chase asked.

London cocked her head. "You mean I didn't tire you out enough this weekend?"

Chase smiled wolfishly. "You gave it a valiant effort."

London chuckled. "Ha-ha. Well my sisters are actually coming to town, so you'll have to give it all you've got again."

"Oh that's right, your half-sisters live in Texas."

"Only Bree lives in Texas. Jada lives in San Francisco."

"I can't wait to meet them."

"Really?"

He grinned. "Don't sound so shocked," Chase replied. "I think I clean up pretty nice."

"Oh that's not it," London said. "I'm not embarrassed for you to meet them. It's just that, well, we've not really defined what *we*," she said, pointing between the two of them, "are, so I wasn't sure if you'd want to meet them."

Chase regarded her. "What would you like us to be London?"

She swallowed visibly. She hadn't expected Chase to throw the question back in her lap. She knew what she wanted them to be, but she also didn't want to scare him off.

"It isn't a trick question," Chase said, teasing her.

"I know that," London finally spoke. "It's just..."

Chase reached for London's coffee mug and placed it on the nightstand beside his. Then he held her hands in his large ones. "Why don't I tell you what I want."

London's shoulders visibly relaxed. "I would like that."

"I want you to be *my* woman. I don't want you to see anyone else, *be* with anyone else."

"You do?"

"There you go doubting me again. What am I going to have to do to convince you I'm legit?"

"Nothing, nothing, nothing," London said. She threw her arms around his shoulders and pulled him into her for a long kiss. "I want that too, Chase. I want to be your lady. And I want you to be *my* man."

"I *am* yours," Chase replied. "I haven't been with another woman since you and I met. Haven't wanted to."

"Wow!" London's hand touched her chest. It meant so much to her that Chase had been celibate this entire time and hadn't gone to another woman looking for what he'd refused to take from her. And now, he wouldn't have to. Since being with Chase, London had come to realize she had a higher-sex drive than she'd originally thought. She'd never been interested in making love several times in an evening, but with Chase, she could go all night long.

Wanted to go all night.

London exulted in the pleasure of feeling so deeply connected to Chase. She wasn't sure how he felt about her just yet, other than that he was staking his claim, but she knew they had a connection that went deeper than sex. He'd proven that by abstaining from a sexual relationship with her until he'd earned back her trust.

"I only want you, London." Chase brought her back to

the present away from her musings. "Matter of fact, I want you right now."

He pulled her down onto the bed with him and kissed her senseless.

"How's London?" Mason asked Chase over beers at the end of a long work day. They'd just finished yet another construction job, and had gone over to a bar. "She looked smashing the other night at the gala."

Chase's chest puffed out. "Thanks, man. She did look pretty hot." He took a swig of his beer.

"I wasn't the only one noticing," Mason said. He tapped the top of his bottle to let the bartender know he wanted another Corona.

"Oh yeah?"

"I caught that slimy ex-husband of hers giving her the once-over," Mason said. "He's probably missing what he used to have."

"Too bad for him," Chase said, tipping his bottle back, "because London is my woman now and I don't intend on giving her up."

"So it's gotten pretty serious between you two?"

Chase coughed. "I wouldn't say that, but we have agreed to be monogamous."

"You? Monogamous?" Mason threw back his head and laughed heartily. "That's really rich coming from you. Do you even know how to keep it in your pants?"

Chase rolled his eyes. "Yeah, I do, Mace. I'm not some Neanderthal clubbing women over the head and bringing them back to my lair so I can have my way with them. It's a two-way street."

"Yeah, yeah." Mason swigged his beer. "But are you really prepared to be with just *one* woman."

"If that woman's London?" Chase inquired. "Heck yeah. She's all I'll ever need in the bedroom, if you get my drift." Chase loved London's slightly freaky side and high-sex drive.

Mason lowered his bottle to the bar and covered his ears. "No need to tell me more. I like London and I don't want to start thinking of her like that."

Chase gave him an evil glare. "You'd better not. That's my woman you're talking about."

"In all seriousness," Mason said, grasping his bottle again, "it's good to see you so happy and finally finding your way here."

Chase nodded. "I am."

"And therapy? How's that going? You've been going for what, about a month now? Seen any progress?"

"What's with all the questions?" Chase reached for the bowl of nuts in the center of the bar, grasped a handful, and tossed them in his mouth.

Mason shrugged. "Does it matter? I thought therapy was going well. But if I'm reading your body language and attitude correctly, it's not."

Chase stiffened.

Mason knew him. They'd been together out in the desert for too long with only each other as company not to pick up when something wasn't right.

"Doc Burke was alright, but he had a lot of questions. And not a whole lot of answers," Chase replied. "So I quit therapy."

"And the nightmares?"

"They're still here, though I have to admit the frequency may have decreased a bit, for now."

"So you admit therapy was working?"

Chase turned to glare at his best friend. "Who's to say that's the reason? I've had spells where I've hardly had any episodes."

"So now you think you're cured after a month?" Mason plopped his bottle on the bar. "Dammit, Chase. Why do you have to be so hard-headed? Can't you get out of your own way long enough to get some help?"

"Hey, hey," Chase said, stepping backward, "where's all this anger coming from? I thought you were on my side."

"I AM ON YOUR SIDE," Mason yelled, "but you have to help me help you. Do you think it was easy for me to get where I am now without losing my wife and kids? Hell no. I had to do the work, Chase. And so do you. You need to get your ass back to therapy."

"Maybe therapy isn't for everyone," Chase returned. "I survived twenty years in the military and I'm still standing. I haven't gone off the rails."

"Not yet," Mason muttered underneath his breath.

"I'm telling you, Mace, it'll all subside." Chase patted his friend's shoulder. "I have this all under control. You'll see."

Chapter 14

"L ONDON!" JADA YELLED WHEN SHE saw London waiting outside the airport terminal. "It's so good to see you."

London couldn't help but smile when her younger sister came barreling toward her with outstretched arms. As London returned her sister's embrace, she was envious that she didn't have Abigail Hart's genes instead of her mother Loretta's.

At five foot nine and weighing no more than a buck twenty-five soaking wet, London was a bit envious of Jada's killer figure. London caught sight of several men openly ogling her in the off-the-shoulder romper she wore. What wasn't there to like? She was legs and then some. Jada's shoulder length hair had just the right tousled look and her hazelnut skin glowed. The sisters embraced.

"Ditto that," Bree said from behind them in the terminal doorway, echoing Jada's sentiments about being happy to see London.

Bree had Jada's same coloring, but she was the exact opposite of Jada, who was all things girly. Bree was a rough-and-tumble tomboy. She wore some faded blue jeans, a camel-colored button-down shirt, some distressed cowboy boots, and carried a duffle bag. Her hair was in its natural state of unruly curls. She looked every bit the role of cowgirl, but then she *had* been raised by Duke.

When Jada finally released her, London walked toward Bree, who immediately dropped her bags and gave London a hug. Though not as tall as Jada, Bree nearly reached London's shoulder.

"Good to see you, sis." Bree pulled away from London. "You're looking good. Happiness agrees with you."

London touched her cheek. "Is it that obvious?"

"Absolutely. You're glowing. So let's get going because I'm eager to hear the dish."

Five minutes later, after London had stored Bree's duffel and Jada's designer luggage into the trunk of her Jeep, they set off toward the city. Their first stop: Shay's.

The lunch rush was just ending, so they'd have plenty of time to get some food and catch up before London was due back to check on the dinner rush. With her sisters in town, she didn't intend on staying at work the entire night, but she did want to poke her head in. Her sisters would have to wait to meet Chase on Sunday. He'd been insistent that she spend Saturday with them.

Once Bree and Jada were seated at a corner table, London brought over a pitcher of sangrias for them and one of her waitresses came out to take the rest of their order. "Do you know what you guys want to have for lunch?" London asked when she sat down across from them at the four-seater.

"Just a bowl of gumbo for me," Jada said.

Bree rolled her eyes. "Well some of us are not watching our figure and considering I work out in the field, I need more calories so I'll have the energy I need."

London turned to her waitress, but she patted her shoulder. "I've got this, boss." Smiling, London turned around to find two pair of eyes staring at her.

"So where is he?" Jada asked, glancing around London's establishment.

"Yeah, when do we get to meet him?"

London feigned ignorance. "Meet who?"

166

"The man whose put that smile on your face," Jada said. "Don't play stupid."

"You'll get a chance to meet Chase before you leave," London said with a grin.

Bree gave her a discerning look. "Are you trying to keep him away from us?"

"Of course not," London said. "I want you to get to know my man."

Jada and Bree looked at each other. *"Your man?"*

London blushed but didn't back down. "You heard right. Chase is my man and he wanted us to have some sisterly bonding time together. So he'll see you tomorrow."

"How gracious of him," Bree replied, "but let him know that he can't escape us because I have a ton of questions for him."

They all laughed and the rest of the lunch continued in the same lighthearted and cheery mood it had started, with her sisters enjoying their lunch and praising the cook until the subject of their father came up.

"And how is Duke?" London inquired.

"He's good," Bree answered, "but he'd love to see you. You should come to Dallas."

"Duke knows where I live," London replied. "If he wants to see me, he can come here."

"Same as us?" Bree quipped.

London rolled her eyes. "That's not fair, Bree. You suggested this trip after Caleb's wedding in an effort to bridge the gap between us as sisters."

"Yes I did," Bree agreed. "I know it hasn't been easy for you, London, always feeling like you're left out or that you're missing out on something."

"I did miss out, Bree. I missed out on having Duke in my life, but it is what it is. I can't make him be present in my life or give a shit about what happens to me."

"Daddy loves you, London," Jada responded hotly. "He

doesn't love you any less than he does us. Or even Trent for that matter. It's just different."

"Whatever." London shrugged. "Why are we talking about this?"

"Because you haven't made your peace with it, London," Bree commented, reaching for her glass of sangria and taking a sip. "And as much as I don't want to throw shade, it's not all Daddy's fault, you know."

London's head whirled around. "What the hell is that supposed to mean?"

Bree faced her head-on. "I'm saying that your mother played a role too in your lack of a relationship by not telling Daddy of your existence. All I'm saying London is that it takes two. All your blame can't be put on one person."

Bree wasn't wrong. London had come to the very same conclusion, but she didn't like hearing it just the same. It was one thing to call your own mama out on the carpet, but it was quite another to have someone else do it, especially someone who didn't know her.

"It's getting late and I'm sure you're both a bit jet-lagged." London rose to her feet. "Plus I have to go in the back to check on dinner service."

"You're not having dinner with us later?" Disappointment was evident in Jada's question.

"Yes, I'll come get you both a little later. I just have to make sure the night starts off right."

"If that's the only reason," Bree said from underneath her breath.

"What was that?"

"Oh nothing," Bree said. "I think that's a fine idea. We'll take a cab to the hotel, check in, rest up for dinner, and of course see Bourbon Street."

London was glad Bree mentioned the infamous street because that turned Jada's focus on what they could see and do while out on the town. Deep down, though, she knew it was Bree's way of trying to avoid yet another disagreement between them.

It's why, after she'd checked on her staff as they prepared for dinner service, she called Violet to see if she wanted to join them for girl's night out.

"I would love to," Violet responded, "but isn't this weekend all about you and your sisters?"

"Yes."

"But there's a 'but' in there."

"Ding. Ding. Ding." London mimicked the sound of a doorbell.

"What's wrong, London? I thought you got along with Bree and Jada."

London sighed. "I do, but every time I see them the conversation turns to Duke, and then it's all downhill."

"My advice would be to figure out how to carve out your own relationship with them separate from your father."

"That's easier said than done."

"You have to try, otherwise all this effort you're putting into attempting to get closer to your sisters will all be for naught."

"I just feel so much closer to you, Violet, than them."

"Aww, thanks sweetie. And you know I love you to pieces, but I think I'm going to sit this one out and allow you, Jada, and Bree to get to know each other."

"But it won't be as much fun on Bourbon Street without you."

"*You're* going to wicked row?" Violet laughed out loud. "Now this I have to see. Maybe I'll meet you down there for a drink."

"Promise?"

"I'll think about it. You twisted my arm," Violet answered. "I hope your sweet and innocent sisters are prepared for a night of debauchery."

London laughed as she got off the phone. She had just enough time to head home, shower, and change for dinner.

In the car as she headed over to her sisters' hotel, she tried to reach Chase, but to her dismay, he didn't pick up.

London was sad.

She hadn't talked to him all day, which was unusual. His typical MO was to check in with her. She just hoped that everything was alright.

When she arrived at her sisters' hotel, they were both standing outside on its main walkway. Jada, ever the fashionista, was dressed in an embellished black bandage dress while Bree was surprisingly stylish in a cold-shoulder flowy white blouse and white jeans. The only other time London could recall Bree in a dress had been during Caleb's wedding festivities.

"Hop in, gals," London said as they climbed into the Jeep. "We have a fun night ahead."

London had made a reservation at one of the finest French restaurants in town thanks to her connections in the industry. And now they were seated at one of the best tables in the house as the maître d brought them over a bottle of the best wine, compliments of the chef.

"This is wonderful, London," Jada gushed. "You shouldn't have gone through all the trouble."

"It was no trouble really. I know Chef Andre. He stopped by Shay's incognito one day and was so enamored with my food that he had to meet me. And the next thing you know, we were fast friends. So when I told him my family was coming to town and I wanted to take them to a great restaurant other than Shay's, he agreed."

"I'm with Jada on this," Bree said, glancing around at the ornate décor in the ages-old restaurant. "This place is phenomenal."

"There's a lot of places like this in New Orleans," London said. "I think that's why I love the city so much.

170

The new and the old come together to create something unique that you can't find anywhere else."

London's phone vibrated beside her on the table and her entire face brightened when she saw who was calling: Chase. She turned her head slightly and lowered her voice several octaves as she answered it. "Hey, honey."

"How's my girl? How's your visit with your sisters?"

London glanced up and saw that Jada and Bree were listening to her conversation with rapt attention. "Ummmm, good, we just sat down to dinner. Where were you earlier?"

"At the gym. Had to let off some steam."

"Oh, alright. Well, uh, are we still on for you to meet my sisters tomorrow?"

"Of course, babe. Where shall I meet you?"

"At church."

"See you then, hugs and kisses."

"Hugs and kisses," she whispered quietly as she ended the call.

"You're sounding quite love-dovey over there," Jada teased. "Does Chase feel the same way about you?"

"What do you mean?"

"You're in love with him," Jada stated. "It's written all over your face. Does he know? Has he said those three little words back?"

London's stunned look caused Bree to elbow Jada in the ribs.

"Oh!" Jada's hand flew to her mouth. "I'm ahead of myself. I'm so sorry. I just assumed..."

Bree stepped in to smooth the waters since London couldn't think of a single thing to say. She'd been trying to keep her feelings for Chase to herself, but it was obvious she wasn't doing a very good job of it.

"How long have you and Chase been seeing each other?" Bree asked.

"Nearly two months."

"See," Bree said, turning to Jada and giving her a wink, "it's much too soon to be talking the 'L' word. Let London enjoy this time with Chase."

"Of course," Jada concurred. "New love is always so exciting." Then she covered her mouth with her hand again. "Oops."

London let out a soft laugh. "It's alright, Jada. I guess my feelings toward Chase are more transparent than I thought."

"So you do love him?"

"Jada!" Bree admonished.

"It's okay," London responded softly. "Yes, I'm in love with Chase, but as Bree said, it's still so new that I don't want to complicate our relationship if he's not there yet. So we're taking it slow and easy."

"Slow and easy is great," Bree concurred.

"And you would know," Jada returned. "When was your last date, Miss Workaholic?"

Bree rolled her eyes. "I'm building my career and that takes time."

"If you want marriage and babies, you'd better hop to it, old girl. You're not getting any younger," Jada commented.

Bree huffed. "I'm only thirty."

"With no prospects," Jada added.

"And what about you, Jada?" London joined their light jesting. "You seeing anyone?"

"No one in particular."

"Because she can never settle on just one," Bree said. "Our sister is a playa. She loves playing the field. You should see her cell phone. It's where the names of men go to the graveyard."

"Ha-ha," Jada said, "at least I have a social life."

"And I'll get one," Bree returned, "all in due time."

The waitress appeared with their entrees and London and her sisters dived in to delicious dishes of wood-fired redfish and snapper. After dinner, Chef Andre came out to talk to them about his inspiration and treated them all to his Bananas Foster. After indulging in that amazing dessert, they all sat back against the booth drinking cappuccinos.

"Who said we were going out to Bourbon Street," Jada said, "because I'm not sure I can move from this table."

"I did," Bree replied, "and we have to. We can't come all the way to New Orleans and at least not walk it."

London excused herself to go to the ladies' room to call Violet. "So, diva, are you still joining us for debauchery on Bourbon Street?" Her voice was filled with excitement at the chance to have fun with her bestie and her sisters.

"Girl, I'm in my pajamas with a pint of Häagen-Dazs," Violet responded. "I'm not going anywhere except to my bed."

"But I thought you were going to come with?"

"Are you or are you not having fun with your sisters?"

London smiled as she thought about the two wonderful women sitting in the main dining room waiting for her. "I am."

"Then you don't need me," Violet said. "Have fun. And call me tomorrow with details. That's if I'm not in a diabetic coma from all this sugar."

"Sure thing, my friend. I'll see you soon."

London, Bree, and Jada hit the town. They stopped to stare at the interesting characters and tourists, watched a male revue show at one of the newest hot spots, and shared a hurricane in the middle of the street. Eventually, London returned them to their hotel in the wee hours of the morning before making it back home. Before she closed her eyes for much needed sleep, she prayed that her sisters would like Chase.

Chapter 15

LONDON NEEDN'T HAVE WORRIED. WHEN she and her sisters met up with Chase hours later, he knocked their socks off. Their love affair with her military man started when he met them outside church before Sunday morning worship.

Chase was looking spectacularly handsome in pressed slacks and a sports jacket over a starched white shirt. He looked casual yet appropriate to attend the worship service. Chase greeted both sisters with a warm hug and a kiss.

"You must be Jada," he said, and wrapped her younger sister into a big bear hug.

Jada smiled and returned his hug.

And when Bree proceeded to offer him her hand instead, he merely enveloped her into his embrace, picking up all five foot six inches of her. When he finally set her back down, he'd made Bree a believer too.

Bree mouthed to London, *He's a keeper.*

Afterward, they went into the church and all sat together, along with London's grandparents, as the minister gave his Sunday sermon. Interestingly enough, it was on being mindful of the pleasures of the flesh. Jada and Bree nudged London and she had to do everything in her power to keep a straight face and not look at Chase. She knew what they must be thinking: That there was no way, with a man as fine as Chase, that she wasn't hitting it every morning, noon, and night.

And if she had her way, she would.

Sex with Chase was different than it had been with Shawn. With Chase, it was fraught with hunger and passion, leaving her trembling in its aftermath. Somewhere along the way, she'd started to care for him—more than that, she'd fallen in love with him. So to her the act wasn't just sex anymore, they were making love. And because of it, she eagerly gave her body to him time and time again.

She was hoping that someday Chase might come to feel about her the way she felt for him.

Today was a start.

Chase waited with her sisters while London said her goodbyes to her grandparents outside the church.

"So," Grandpa Jeremiah said, inclining his head toward Chase, Bree, and Jada, who were huddled in a group nearby, "things seem to be progressing between the two of you."

London smiled. "Yes, they have."

"And that pleases you?"

"Of course, Grandpa. I wouldn't let him meet Bree and Jada otherwise."

"I was happy to see those young'uns here today," he responded.

"Did you expect that Duke Hart raised a bunch of hellions?"

"Considering what I know about the man," he replied, "I wouldn't be surprised, but no. I actually meant that I'm happy to see that they are here to see you, support you. That's a wonderful thing they're doing."

London turned to stare back at her sisters. "Yes, it is."

"Well, I won't keep you any longer, but stop by after they've left. I wanna hear about their visit."

"Sure thing, Grandpa." She waved at him, gave her grandmother a quick kiss, and rushed off toward the group.

"Ready for brunch?" she asked cheerily.

"Lead the way," Bree said.

Chase reached for her hand and together they walked toward their vehicles.

Chase was feeling pretty good about how the day with London and her sisters was progressing. The initial meeting at church had gone well and brunch had gone swimmingly. They'd even retired to a nearby hole in the wall that played jazz on Sundays. Now, they were sitting out on the terrace under an umbrella drinking mojitos as they listened to the sounds of a darn good jazz quartet.

Chase found Jada to be a breath of fresh air with her youthful appeal and sweet innocence. Bree, on the other hand, was a real ballbuster. He could see her giving the man in her life a run for the money in regards to who was going to wear the pants in *that* relationship.

Luckily for him, London was every bit a lady. He loved not only her womanly curves, her round behind, and the fullness of her overabundant breasts, but he also appreciated the softness of her character and the way she had her own opinion but never diminished him or made him feel less than a man despite of all his issues.

The PTSD hadn't gotten any better since he'd stopped seeing Dr. Burke. In fact, it seemed to have gotten worse. The nightmares had resurfaced in the last few days. Chase had been happy that London had her sisters to occupy her time. Otherwise, she would've expected him to stay the night and right now, he couldn't chance it. He didn't want to scare her as he'd done twice before. But he also hadn't figured out how he could make love to her and then leave.

"Chase."

"Hmmm?" He returned his thoughts to the present.

Bree was giving him a stern glare. "I hope we're not boring you."

"Not at all, Bree. I apologize. Just have some things on my mind. What did you ask?"

"I asked how long you've been in New Orleans."

"Not quite a year."

"And do you intend to stay?"

Chase glanced across the table at London and reached for her hand. "There's no place I'd rather be."

"So just how serious are you about my sister?"

"Bree, watch yourself," Jada warned.

Chase's ears prickled at her tone, but he let it slide. He knew she was being overprotective and he could appreciate that. He knew better than anyone the job Shawn had done on London and how he'd deflated her self-confidence. It was why he did everything in his power to make sure London knew just how beautiful she was to him, no matter her size.

And of course, he happened to prefer full-figured women.

"I don't mind answering, Jada. I have nothing to hide."

"Glad to hear it," Bree commented.

"And as for London and I, we're still in the getting to know each other stage."

"And what after?"

"What do you mean?"

"Don't act like a man and be dense," Bree said, reaching for her mojito on the table and taking a sip. "You know what I mean."

"If you're asking if I'm open to marriage," Chase said, "I don't know. It hasn't been that long since my divorce."

Instantly, London slipped her hand from his, putting physical distance between them.

And the look in her eyes told Chase he'd hurt her, not intentionally, but he had. He hadn't said it to be hurtful, he was merely being honest. "That's not to say that I wouldn't get married again."

"I see." For once Bree was uncharacteristically quiet. And that's how she was for the remainder of their time at the table, including London. If it wasn't for poor Jada, who did her best to keep the conversation going with funny stories or anecdotes, the rest of the afternoon would have been a bust. Eventually, it was London who stood up to excuse herself to go to the restroom.

Chase rose to his feet too, but Jada immediately jumped up and said, "I'll go with you." She followed London to the ladies' room.

Chase didn't need to be a rocket scientist to know London was upset with him.

"You really stuck your foot in your mouth on that one," Bree said, sitting back in her chair as she regarded him wryly.

He plopped back down in his chair. "Thanks a lot."

"C'mon, Chase, don't tell me you guys haven't talked about where your relationship is headed."

At his silence, Bree sat upright in her chair. "You mean you haven't discussed it?"

He shook his head.

"So today was the first time that London heard you may not be interested in marriage?"

"I'm not saying I'm *not* interested. I love being with London." At Bree's narrowed eyes, he explained, "And not just physically, if that's what you're thinking. I'm committed to her and I've only dated London since I've been in New Orleans."

"But?"

"But I was burned, Bree," Chase admitted, "badly by my ex-wife. It wasn't pretty nor my reaction to my divorce. I'm just not sure I can go down that rabbit hole again."

"And you think London wants to? Shawn was a miserable excuse for a husband, but you," Bree said, "you could be the real deal, and the exact kind of man London should have been with in the first place."

Chase grinned broadly. "Coming from you, that's high praise."

"I don't like a lot of people, Chase, but I like you. And I believe you care about my sister, but you also can't be so gun-shy that you're not willing to step up to the plate when the time comes. And I think that time might be coming sooner than you think."

London and Jada returned to the table.

"London, I was thinking Jada and I are going to head back to the hotel and get packed for our flight tomorrow," Bree said.

Jada glanced down at her watch. "But it's only..." She caught sight of the look in Bree's eyes and didn't finish her sentence. "Sounds like a great idea."

"Alright," London said, "I'll drop you both off."

"No need," Bree returned, rising to her feet. "I called a taxi and it'll be here any minute." Or at least she would once she and Jada departed.

"You don't need to do that," London said. "I don't mind."

"I know, but I'll see you tomorrow. We'll have breakfast before we leave. Alright?"

London nodded.

Bree and Jada quickly left the table and headed for the entrance. "Do you think it worked?" Jada whispered on the way out.

"I sure hope so," Bree whispered, "because he's got to dig his way out of this one on his own."

London stared at her sisters' retreating backs before turning to glare at Chase. "If I didn't know any better, I'd think you told them to get lost."

"I wish I could take the credit, but it wasn't me," Chase said, "though I'm not sorry to see them go because I think we should talk."

"Not here."

"Alright. Where?"

"I'd love to get out of my church clothes, so if you don't mind going back to my place…"

"Your place it is. I'll follow behind you."

Several moments later, they were walking out of the restaurant. London didn't see Bree and Jada hiding in the shadows giving Chase the thumbs-up signal.

With traffic at a minimum on an early Sunday evening, London arrived to her house in no time. The sun was just starting to set when Chase pulled up behind her Jeep and hopped out of his truck.

Silently, he followed her up the pathway to her house and waited as she opened the front door. Once inside, the air was thick with tension. London eased out of her blazer and Chase was right there behind her to help her out of it.

"Thanks."

He set it aside on her foyer table and was quiet as she kicked off her shoes and padded to the living room. She'd like nothing better than to strip out of her Sunday best, but her problem with Chase wasn't in the bedroom. It was outside the bedroom that they needed to work on their communication skills.

"C'mon, London, I know you're upset with me," Chase said once they were seated in the living room.

"Upset? No, I'm more hurt that you haven't shared your thoughts on marriage and the future with me. Why is this the first time I'm hearing that you may not want to ever remarry? And in front of my sisters? It was humiliating."

"London, I never meant to hurt you," Chase began, "but we've never talked about the future. Sure we talked about boundaries and commitment, but for some reason we've both skated around the other topic. It wasn't just me. You've *never* asked me."

"I-I guess I just assumed that you wanted the same things as me," London replied quietly.

"And I'm not saying that I don't," Chase's voice rose. "I'm just saying that I'm confused. I never expected to meet you. I never expected that I would enjoy spending time with you. And that when I wasn't, I'd think of you every waking minute."

"You do?"

"Of course I do." Chase grasped one of her cheeks in his hand. "Baby, I adore you."

London allowed herself to bask in the moment for a few seconds before pulling away. "But you're not sure you want more? You're not sure you want to be with me long term?"

Chase sighed heavily. "Don't put words in my mouth, London. It's not fair. I never said that."

"No, you just said that you were confused and not sure if you would ever remarry. Well guess what, Chase? I'm sure. I'm sure of what I want. I'm sure that now or in the *future*, I want to be with a man who's committed to me one hundred percent and in it for the long haul. Not someone who's looking for an exit strategy or waiting for the next shoe to fall or for me to betray him."

Spinning on her heel, London started toward her bedroom, but she never made it there because Chase caught up to her in the hall.

He hauled her to him, crushing her breasts against his chest. "I have never been waiting for the next shoe to drop, London, because you're not Bianca."

"No?" London cried. "Then why are you punishing me for her sins? Why don't I get a clean slate for you to give me one hundred percent of you, no holds barred? Why don't you tell me what you're thinking? Or what you're feeling after you've had one of those horrible nightmares? Why do you keep me at arm's length?"

"Dammit, London! There's no reason for you to hit below the belt." Chase released her suddenly and she stumbled backward. He began walking toward the door.

"That's right. Run away, Chase, because that's what you do. You run away when you're hurt or upset, instead of staying and toughing it out."

"Is that what I should have done?" Chase asked, turning to look at her. His face was filled with rage. "I should have stayed and been talked down to and cheated on like Shawn did to you?"

"Oh." London clutched her hand over her mouth and rushed down the hall toward her bedroom.

"London, wait." Chase ran after her. He put his shoe in the doorway just as London tried to slam the door. She tried to use her bodyweight to close it, but Chase was too strong and barreled inside her room.

"Baby, I'm sorry. I shouldn't have said that," Chase said.

Tears streamed down London's cheeks. "Why, when it's the truth?" she cried. She sat down, teetering on the edge of her bed. "I was pathetic to stay with him for as long as I did, but you know what? At least I can say I fought for what I wanted even if it didn't work out in the end."

Chase rushed over to London from a bedroom corner. He kneeled at her feet and reached for her hands. "I'm sorry, London. It was a cruel thing to say. I'm sorry. Please forgive me."

London stared down at the floor, unwilling to meet his eyes. "Chase, I think it's just best that you go."

"No, I don't want to leave like this." He squeezed her hand. "Please say you'll forgive me."

London didn't want to look at him because if she did, she knew she wouldn't be immune to him. She couldn't think straight around Chase. So when he reached out and pulled her into his arms and kissed her with the faintest brush of his lips against hers, her instinct took over.

It was a butterfly kiss. Soft and light, but it was enough to set her on fire. And when she felt the tip of his tongue, tantalizingly licking its way to the entrance of her mouth, seeking entry, she let him in. She wanted him to insert that delicious tongue of his inside her mouth and mimic their lovemaking. She melted against him. She was completely defenseless.

Her breasts grew heavy and her sex ached with need. Her hands moved to the corded muscles of his arms and upward to his powerful shoulders. Then she wrapped her arms around his neck.

Chase wasted no time unzipping the back of her dress and it slid to her midriff. Then he slipped his hand inside her bra to finger her nipples. When he deepened the kiss, she moaned aloud. That was all Chase needed to begin undressing her further. And she helped him, tearing at her own clothes and his with shaking hands. When they were both naked, her mouth reached hungrily for his and they fell backward on the bed.

Like a missile, his hands instantly went to where she was hot, moist, and quivering for his touch.

"God, you feel so good, London," Chase said as his thumb circled her clit, back and forth, over and over.

London's desire for Chase was spiraling out of control. So much so that when he pulled away and she heard a zip and tear of a condom foil, she knew she should stop so they could clear the air between them, but she was in the throes of passion and couldn't get off the train.

She opened her eyes long enough to see the hungry look in Chase's eyes as he brought his hard arousal toward her. And then he was back on the bed, positioning himself between her thighs, kissing her. And when he finally entered her, he groaned.

London glimpsed an unfamiliar expression flash in Chase's eyes, but just as quick, it was gone, and he was stroking her with singular precision, finding his rhythm. He thrust into her hard and deep. London opened her mouth to scream, but Chase silenced her with his kisses.

Frantically they reached the pinnacle, her body clenching around his. London bit his shoulder and

Chase cried out her name, tightening his arms around her as spasms overtook him. He held London close until eventually he rolled onto his back.

London was breathless and dazed by their coupling. It had never been like this. They'd been so crazed for one another. Chase had clearly shown her that she wasn't so upset with him that he couldn't still get to her, get *inside* her. She wanted him like she'd wanted no other man.

But where did that leave them really if he wasn't willing to go out on the ledge with her. She couldn't be the only one invested in their relationship. She refused to be that same woman fighting for something that would ultimately fail.

Chapter 16

UNDER THE COVER OF DARKNESS in London's bed, Chase had time to gather his thoughts about what had just happened between the two of them. Their lovemaking just now had been wild and free and the best he'd ever had.

So why was it so hard for him to envision a future with London?

It wasn't.

Not really. He was just scared of what it would mean to really put himself out there. Agreeing to date London exclusively had given him the security she'd needed to move forward with their relationship. Chase had thought they were both in agreement about their arrangement. Until now.

Now London was pushing him for more.

She wanted him to open up to her.

To show her they had a future together.

Chase wasn't sure what the future looked like because he'd never been sure he'd ever live to see it. Despite his marriage to Bianca, for twenty years he'd always known that his next mission with his Special Forces unit could be his last. He'd married Bianca to appease her because she'd wanted a family and kids one day.

Looking back, he could see that he had made the wrong move. He hadn't really been ready for marriage or children and he certainly hadn't had a career that would champion one. And it had cost him dearly.

And now it was happening again. London wanted more from him than maybe he could or was willing to give. His divorce had been painful and made him gun-shy. He couldn't run the risk of heartbreak again.

But isn't the prospect of a life without her much worse?

In their short time together, London had come to mean more to him than any woman ever had, including Bianca. So why was he so afraid to let her in? All the way in? See all his demons?

Because maybe, just maybe, they'd be too much for her and she'd walk away?

Chase was uncertain of what to do. He was not a man given to self-reflection, he was a man of action. If something needed to be done, he did it. He'd learned as a child to be strong. How could he not be when he'd lost his mother at six years old? His father had drummed into him that a man never cried, was never vulnerable, so Chase had crushed his fears down inside and developed a thick skin.

And now London wanted to peel back those layers of skin and get underneath them.

Chase punched his pillow and rolled onto his side away from London's sleeping form. He begged for sleep to overtake him, but it didn't come.

Instead, he dreamt of war.

And man's quenchable lust to conquer new countries and territories—and not just for religion as some thought, but for their own self gain. Peppering his dream were images of Bosnia along with ones of his fallen comrades. He saw himself holding one of the lifeless hands of one of his men as his lifeblood seeped into the hot desert sand. He heard the soldier's dying words to take back to his wife and unborn child. Regret filled Chase's heart as he remembered the guilt and powerlessness.

"Nooo!" Chase yelled and bolted upward with a start.

He glanced around him and realized where he was. He wasn't in Bosnia.

He glanced down at London and she was still sound asleep. He was thankful he'd only screamed in his dreams and not scared her to death.

Slowly, he pushed the covers back and eased out of bed. He would sleep on the couch until morning and return at daybreak before London ever realized he was gone.

Creeping out of the room, he closed the door behind him, unaware that London heard the click of the door and had sat upright.

The next morning, Chase returned to the bed as usual but before he could get settled in good, London stirred beside him. Levering himself up with an elbow, he looked down at her flushed face. "London?"

"Yes?"

"Good morning."

She wiped the sleep from her eyes. "Good morning."

A long uncomfortable silence passed before he said, "Last night was—was incredibly hot."

"Or incredibly stupid," she responded, sitting up and turning on the bedside lamp.

"Stupid?" His eyebrows bunched into a frown.

"It didn't change anything between us," London returned. "It only proved that we have a hard time keeping our hands off each other."

He sat up in the bed and looked straight at her. He didn't like her tone. "And that's a problem? I didn't hear you complaining." All he had heard was her low moans of pleasure as he'd thrust deep inside her.

"You know I'm not talking about sex," London said. "I'm talking about the fact that you won't share with me what's going on with you. That you won't confide in me that you still have nightmares."

"They've all but subsided."

"Really, Chase?" She gave him an incredulous look. "Really? Do I look stupid to you? Do you think I didn't see you creep out of bed when you thought I was sleeping because you were too afraid to sleep beside me?"

How does she know? He'd thought she'd been sleeping.

She nodded and pointed to his face. "There it is. The truth, finally. I'm not blind, Chase. I know you're hurting, but you refuse to let me in. Why won't you let me in?"

"Because," he said as he threw back the covers and searched the room for his trousers, "this has nothing to do with you London, with us."

"Bullshit! It has everything to do with us, Chase, especially if we can't sleep together like a normal couple."

"Well, I'm sorry if I'm not *normal* enough for you, London. Excuse me if I endured hell in six tours and have just a few battle scars." Chase found his trousers on the floor and put one leg and then the other in them and zipped them up.

"Don't you dare." She kneeled on her shins on the bed. "Don't you dare make this about your service. I *want* to understand what you've been through, but you won't tell me. You only give me bits and pieces."

"Because, London, it's my truth," Chase pounded his chest. "It's my truth."

"No, it's your demons, Chase," London returned. "Demons you won't face. Have you ever thought about getting help?"

"Why? Do you think I'm cuckoo for Cocoa Puffs." Chase spun his index finger around his temple as he glanced around the room for his shirt. Not finding it, he nixed the T-shirt and began dressing without it.

Tears sprung to London's eyes, "Of—of course not." She crawled toward him and pushed his hands away so she could button his collared shirt for him. "I've never thought that, but I think you might need to talk to someone about whatever is eating you up inside and prevents you from sleeping."

"I've never needed much sleep."

She threw her hands up in the air. "There you go again, making light of this. This is serious, Chase. You need help."

He folded his arms across his chest. "And if I don't get it?"

"Then I don't know if we're going to make it," London replied. "Is that what you want? Is this your way of pushing me away without telling me to take a hike, 'cause if so, just say so."

"This isn't about you, London! Or about us. It's about me. Don't you get it? There are parts of me you won't ever know completely."

"I don't know if I can accept that."

Chase picked his shoes up from the floor and turned to toward the door. "Then I guess you're going to have to decide if you're going to take me or leave me. If you take me, you'll have to decide if you're willing to accept me as I am with all my flaws because I'm not sure if I'm capable of giving you any more."

Chase's words lingered long after he left that morning and London had said goodbye to her sisters at the airport. Later that same day, she went about her normal Monday duties at Shay's: checking and ordering supplies, writing out checks, and balancing the restaurant's finances. But despite how busy she was, London was still thinking of Chase and the terrible row they'd had.

And to make matters worse, Chase didn't call or text her that day. London hadn't realized just how much she'd come to look forward to his calls or texts to start her day until they were MIA.

Am I so wrong in wanting him to get help?

He was clearly struggling, but he refused her help and apparently anyone else's. She was at a loss. And whenever she had a lot on her mind, she stopped by her grandfather's. He always had sage advice that usually led her down the right path.

And she had a few hours before lunch and dinner to call on him.

She found her grandfather in his garden, pruning his prized roses. He'd bought the rose bush for her grandma many years ago, but that hadn't stopped him from ensuring that each year the bushes bloomed. They were important to him. He always wanted to put a dozen of them on his wife's table every wedding anniversary.

"Baby girl." Grandpa Jeremiah looked up when he heard the crackling sound of her footsteps on the concrete by the side of the house. "What are you doing here during the middle of the day?"

"Hoping for some one-on-one time with you if you're free," London said.

"I'm always free for you." He put his shears and gloves in his apron pocket. "Come to the porch and we'll have some lemonade and cookies while we talk. Your grandma just made a new batch."

The last thing London needed was more cookies to add to her already full frame, but she had never been able to turn down her grandma's famous chocolate chip cookies and today wouldn't be any different.

Grandpa Jeremiah entered the house for the cookies and returned with several on separate plates. He sat on the loveseat on the wraparound porch, where London joined him. He turned to her with a cookie in his hand. "What's on your mind?"

"I need some advice on men."

"Well, I am one so I suppose I can help," he said with a chuckle, laughing at his own joke.

"You know, Chase and I have been seeing each other the last few months."

"I told you that young man was a fine catch."

London smiled at his patting himself on the back. "He is. I don't doubt that, but he is troubled, Grandpa."

"Probably saw too much war," her grandfather replied. "Happened to some of my friends. After they were drafted for Vietnam, when they got back, they were never the same. But Chase doesn't strike me as a man of weak disposition."

"He isn't." London shook her head fervently. "I think he's being too strong by not admitting that he's hurting."

"How so?"

"He suffers terrible nightmares, Grandpa. They have him waking up screaming."

Grandpa Jeremiah frowned. "Has he hurt you, child?"

"No, never, and that's not why I'm telling you this. I'm just trying to figure out how to get him to see that he needs to talk to someone, a professional, to sort through all the hurt and the pain. And maybe, just maybe, make peace."

"That sounds like a whole lot of maybes. What if he finds no peace? What then? Are you prepared to let him go?"

London didn't even know what to think of that alternative because she wouldn't, couldn't, lose Chase. She loved him.

"Ah, there's the rub," Grandpa Jeremiah stated. "You can't let him go because you love him. But what you have to realize, baby girl, is that love doesn't always come in a nice, neat little package."

"I know that. Remember Shawn?"

"Of course I do, but isn't Chase worth a hundred Shawns and look how long you stayed with that knucklehead and fought for him."

London nodded in agreement. He had a point there. She'd done everything in her power to save their marriage even though she should have thrown in the towel much sooner. It had taken his boldness with showcasing his affair with that harlot in public to make London finally see the light.

Didn't Chase deserve the same loyalty? Shouldn't she try just as hard to fight for what they had? It might be imperfect, but she was certain that Chase cared for her and dare she hope, *loved her.*

She grabbed one of the cookies from the plate on her lap and began munching. "You've given me a lot to think about."

"Don't think too long and let dust settle, otherwise Chase may think you've abandoned him. And after the little bit you've told me, it could be the final straw for him."

Chapter 17

CHASE PUNCHED THE BOXING BAG repeatedly, circling it again and again.

"You alright, Chase?" Norm, the gym owner, asked when Chase didn't let up his relentless pounding of the bag.

Chase stopped long enough to glare at him. "I'm fine."

"If that bag could talk, it might disagree."

"Yeah, well, I have a lot to work out." Chase did a quick jab-jab and the bag went swinging.

"Wanna talk about it?"

Chase caught the bag. "Why the hell does everyone think that talking about shit makes it better? It doesn't help. No offense, but I don't want to talk. I just want to be left alone."

"Sure thing, man." Norm nodded. "I'll leave you to it."

Chase let go of the bag and stared at Norm's retreating figure. Norm didn't deserve his hostility. From what he'd seen since his arrival to town, Norm had an open-door gym policy for veterans as a thank you for their service. Chase appreciated being able to come here whenever he needed to blow off some steam.

And today was one of those days.

He hadn't spoken to London in two days and it was killing him.

He missed her.

But he didn't miss her relentless needling and asking him to talk about his feelings. He'd been there done that and therapy had only made him angry. Dr. Burke had always wanted him to look backward at his past in the military, his failed marriage to Bianca, and sometimes even further back at the death of his mother when he was six or losing his father to colon cancer when he was nearly twenty-three.

Chase could still remember getting that call during the middle of the night when he'd been stationed in Germany. His recent purchase of a grandfather clock had failed to chime, which had been unusual, and then the call had come from his superior that they needed to see him back at the base and to be ready to leave.

He hadn't known what it was all about. Certainly his unit hadn't been called back into combat—he would have heard about that from his buddy Mason. But he'd done as he was told and immediately rushed to dress in his uniform and pack his gear in his duffel bag. What he hadn't been expecting was for his company commander to tell him that his father was in the ICU or that the Red Cross would have a ticket waiting for him at the airport.

When he'd arrived at the hospital back in the States, his father was in bad shape. He'd lost nearly fifty pounds since he'd been on chemotherapy and the doctors told Chase it wouldn't be long now before Myles Tanner met Chase's mother in heaven. Chase had been upset to learn that his father had been ill for some time and hadn't told him. Thankfully he'd arrived in time to spend those last few weeks of his father's life with him. They'd even gone to his favorite seafood spot and peeled fresh garlic shrimp and cracked crab legs together.

Chase would never forget those moments.

But what good did it do to look back? It didn't help with the nightmares or make him a better man for London. Instead, he was just as screwed up as before, if not worse.

196

How did he get London to see that? All he needed, all he wanted, was her. In time, she would be enough to help rid him of the pain. But was it fair to put all that pressure on London to ease the pain in his heart? In his soul?

So he stayed away.

Chase told himself it was for London, but it was for him too. He wasn't sure he could bare to see the sad look in her eyes when he failed to be the man she needed and give her everything her heart desired. And if he tried, Chase was scared of what would be unleashed from him if he did. Some secrets, some hurts, some pains were better left in the closet.

If he let them out, acknowledged them, gave them credence, Chase doubted he'd ever be able to close the door. *Then what?* He would be left to deal with it all. And that scared the hell out of him.

He punched the boxing bag again. Again. Again.

Half an hour later, Chase was still miserable. Punishing himself at the gym had done little to alleviate his anxiety. He couldn't go on like this. He needed to see London. Try and talk things out and see if they could come to some sort of ceasefire until they figured out what they would do.

So he decided to drive to Shay's. Dinner service hadn't started, so Chase was hoping he could talk to London if only to clear the air. He just prayed she would be willing to listen.

London sat at one of the tables in the front of the house and poured over several recipes. She had a few ideas that she wanted to try out. Back in the day, if Shawn had been around he would have told her to stick with what she knew. *Cook Southern and Creole food, that's what tourists come to expect from The Big Easy, why mess with a good thing?* he'd say.

But London had gone to culinary school after Tulane

and her foray into the business world, and there was so much more to her than down-home cooking. She was drinking a glass of sweet tea when she heard the restaurant door chime.

"We're not open," London said. She was so engrossed in her recipe cards that she didn't bother looking up from them.

"If that's how you treat your customers, no wonder you always had trouble keeping patrons in our establishment," a masculine voice said.

London glanced up and stared at Shawn. He was looking well-groomed as always in a dress shirt and trousers. Her brows furrowed. "First of all, this is *my* establishment, which I paid you very handsomely for in the divorce. Second, what the hell are you doing here, Shawn?"

He smiled devilishly. "Can't I look up an old friend?"

London snorted. "We were never friends, Shawn."

"Lovers then?"

"If I recall," London said, rising to her feet, "we weren't much of that either." She hadn't liked that Shawn was staring down at her. At least standing, she nearly equaled him in height if not size.

Shawn didn't back away though. Instead he gave her the once-over as he'd done at the gala. His eyes traveled over her peplum ruffled tank top and stretch jacquard crop pants.

"What?" London was annoyed at his frank assessment of her, as if he had the right to look at her that way. She didn't like it one damn bit. That right was reserved for Chase, whether he wanted it right now or not.

Her stubborn pride had made her wait to see if Chase would call her first, but he hadn't. It had now been two days since she'd last seen him, since they'd last made love, and she was torn. Should she make the first move like her grandfather had suggested?

"There's something different about you," Shawn said, circling her, "and I just can't put my finger on it."

"I've probably put on a few pounds," she muttered. As soon as the words were out of her mouth, London wanted to take them back. It was just like her to put herself down whenever she was around Shawn. *Why am I falling into old patterns?*

Shawn shook his head and took a step back. "No, it's not that. And if I didn't know any better, I'd say you've lost a few, which is surprising considering how I begged you to go on a diet."

Ah, and there it was. An infamous Shawn putdown. "Maybe I never felt like you were worth the trouble."

"And this new brotha is?" Shawn inquired. "He got you so sprung that you're willing to put down the fried chicken?"

"You're despicable, Shawn," London said and leaned over the table to reach for the recipe cards. She placed them back in the box. "And I'm well rid of you."

"Oh, c'mon London." Shawn came around the table to help her pack up the recipes. "Don't go getting all offended now. That's how we've always been with each other."

"You're wrong, Shawn. That's how you were with *me.*" She snatched the recipes from his hand and dropped them in the box. She walked over to a nearby chest and put them inside and then turned around to face him. When she did, she noticed he'd been watching her backside. "You never resisted a moment to put me down or make feel bad about my weight. Well guess what? I don't care what you think of me anymore."

"Because you have a new man?" Shawn inquired. He strolled toward her until he was only a few feet away, blocking her path. "What's he got that I don't?"

"A heart. I believe yours froze over a long time ago where I was concerned. I believe that's when you decided to take a *lover.* You know the one I'm talking about, the skinny heifer you had at the gala."

"Still jealous?"

"Of her?" London chuckled. "She can have your sorry ass. That shipped sailed for me a long time ago when I realized I deserved better than you."

"Better than me?" Shawn asked, puffing out his chest. "That dude looks like the only thing he can do is sling a hammer. You were never into the jock types."

"No, I was into pretty boys like you and look were that got me. Chase is ten times the man you'll ever be."

"Oh yeah?" Shawn walked toward London, pushed her backward, and forced her up against a chest. "I don't think so, London." He caressed her cheek. "Despite all your bravado, I don't think you've ever really gotten over me. I mean, how could you... I was the man who married you."

Chase stood dumbfounded as he stared through the window of Shay's at the scene unfolding in front of him. He didn't know what made him peek inside. Maybe he'd been scared to face London and wanted to see if the coast was clear.

He hadn't expected to find her cuddled up with her ex Shawn in the middle of the afternoon. The man was all over his woman! His woman! He punched his fist in his hand. He was ready to go knock his lights out, but he paused.

Did London still think of herself as his woman? Or had she already given up on him and decided to go back to Shawn's lying ass? Had he really gotten it all wrong? Was London like his ex-wife Bianca and incapable of being faithful? Were all women?

Chase moved away from the window and leaned against the building. A sharp pain seared his chest. Betrayed. Again. *How could I have been so stupid to think London wanted me over that slick playboy? I'm just a retired military veteran with not much of a real career, but Shawn?*

Chase had seen how spiffy the man was dressed at the gala and today was no different. He was sure the BMW parked in front of Shay's was his. What could he really offer London? Except his love.

Love.

The word was symbolic because right now Chase knew that's how he felt about London. It had taken seeing her with her ex-husband to make him realize he was in love with her. *Why couldn't I have seen that two days ago?* he wondered as pain roiled in his gut.

Because he was a fool who was destined to be alone.

Heartbroken, Chase stormed back to this truck and drove away.

"Back off, Shawn." London didn't like that Shawn was in her personal space, and if she wasn't mistaken, trying to put the moves on her and cheat on the skinny heifer as he'd done on her.

"C'mon, London," Shawn murmured. "Don't act like you don't want none of this," he said, motioning down his body. "If I recall, you used to like to ride me quite often."

"Whenever you weren't putting me down and calling me fat or making me feel useless."

He frowned. "I never called you fat."

"No? Or maybe you just insinuated that I wasn't on your level and worthy to be on your arm. But it doesn't matter anyway, Shawn, because I'm with Chase now and we have no problems in the bedroom. He knows how to put it on me so good that we can go all night long."

Shawn straightened, standing upright. "All night long, huh?"

London gave him a devilish smile. "Oh yeah. You might think he's only good for manual labor, but that's the thing, Shawn. Because of it, he has stamina for days unlike you, who was only good for once a night if that."

"Perhaps if you hadn't started packing on the pounds I would have had a higher-sex drive."

"Ha, and there it is," London said, "one of your infamous putdowns. I don't even think you realize you're saying them. Luckily for me, I don't measure my self-worth through your eyes. Get out, Shawn."

"London, I'm sorry. I shouldn't have said that," Shawn quickly apologized. "I just didn't like hearing about you and your new man, but I'm really digging this new you. You're more confident and vocal. Where was this woman when we were married?"

London stared back at Shawn. She wish she'd known, because this was who she was but for some reason when she'd been with Shawn she'd taken a backseat to him and lost her voice.

And she'd never go back to being that weak, spineless woman again. Losing Shawn had inspired her to find herself and the man she was meant to be with: Chase.

"Honestly, Shawn, I don't know where she was, but she's here now and she ain't going nowhere," London responded. "But you are." She glanced down at her watch. "I have to get ready for dinner service."

"So that's it? After everything we shared?"

"How you can say that with a straight face after you walked away from our marriage amazes me, but yes that's it. There's nothing here for you, Shawn. Go back and cozy up to that skinny heifer you loved so much."

"Alright, London. I'll leave." Shawn started toward the door, but stopped midstride. "Just so you know, I don't love her, how could I, after I had you?"

Seconds later, he was walking out of the front door.

Where the hell did that come from? London wondered. If she'd heard that shit a year ago when she'd still been down in the dumps, she might have believed him, wanted to believe him. But this year had given her clarity and she knew that Shawn didn't love anyone but himself.

She, however, was in love with Chase. And she would tell him so just as soon as the night was over.

Dinner service had been so busy, London didn't get a moment's peace, let alone a chance, to call Chase and have a serious talk about the state of their relationship. She hated that she'd allowed the day to go by without clearing the air between them and letting him know how she felt.

Standing under a long hot shower, London was dying to share with him her true feelings. She had loved him for some time and had been carrying it around with her, but now that she'd made the decision to tell him she was ready to shout it from the rooftops.

But it was nearly eleven p.m. on Wednesday, and London knew just how early Chase got up for work: five a.m. She didn't dare wake him up. She would just have to wait yet another day. She could only pray that he wouldn't reject her love.

Chapter 18

"CHASE, GET YOUR HEAD OUT of your ass," the foreman yelled at him Thursday afternoon.

Chase glared at the man. He didn't appreciate being talked to like he was some guy off the street. He knew how to do this job better than the foreman did. During his time in the military, he'd helped build many a bridge, village, hell, dozens of homes, but his head wasn't in it today. Not after yesterday.

Not after he'd seen London cozying up to her ex-husband in the middle of the afternoon! When anyone could have walked in on them.

Chase had thought about confronting the lying duo to their faces, but he didn't want a repeat of what had happened between him, Bianca, and his former best friend, Owen. Upon finding Bianca and Owen in their marital bed, Chase had damn near beat Owen to a pulp, until eventually Bianca had flagged down a couple of their neighbors on the base. It had taken two men to pull him off and avoid killing the man.

That's how Chase had felt yesterday when he'd seen London and Shawn together. He'd seen red. It had taken everything in Chase not to go after him. And what of London? He'd done his best to do right by her. Sure, he'd messed up in the beginning, but he'd redeemed himself by courting her, showing her that she was more than a piece of ass.

Didn't she realize that's all she would ever be to Shawn? Shawn didn't really want her back. He just didn't want anyone else to have her. It killed Chase to think she didn't feel the same way about him that he felt about her.

He'd certainly tried to avoid his feelings by keeping her at arm's length, but try as he might, London had chipped away at his armor until he'd finally opened his heart and allowed her in—allowed love in. But where did that leave him now?

His future looked bleak and uncertain.

"Chase, did you hear me?" the foreman yelled again, getting up in Chase's face.

Chase replied in an ice-cold tone, "I heard you the first damn time. Now get out of my face and let me do my job."

"Do you know who you're talking to?"

"Yeah, I do," Chase said. "I'm not one of these kids"— he pointed to several workers standing nearby listening to their exchange—"who's wet behind the ears and need you to lead them around by the hand. I've got this. So let me do it."

"Of all the—" The foreman started toward him and on reflex Chase grabbed his arm and turned it upward, forcing the man to the ground on his knees.

"Chase!" Mason came running toward him as Chase prepared to give the foreman a can of whoop ass. He was in no mood for bullshit today. "Let him go."

Chase instantly released the man, who clutched his wrist.

"What the hell was that?" the foreman yelled. "You could have broken my wrist and how would I feed my family?"

"You should have thought about that before you attacked ex-Special Forces," Mason replied. "He could have killed you with his bare hands, same as me."

"You guys are both pretty deadly!" the foreman yelled. "Why don't you both take a load off for the day?"

"You're sending us both home?" Mason inquired with a growl. "I didn't do anything."

"You took his side, so now you can both go commiserate over a beer as you take the day *unpaid*." The foreman turned on his heel and walked away.

"That son of a bitch!" Mason stumped his foot in the sand. "That's what I get for helping your sorry ass even after you've been an asshole all day."

Chase smiled. "Me? An asshole?" Though he knew Mason was right. All day he'd been on a tear; the foreman had just lit his fuse. He was sorry Mason was paying the price though. "Listen, Mace, I'm sorry. I'll pay you back the day's wages."

"Whatever." Mason snatched off his hard hat and began walking toward his truck.

"Wait up." Chase ran after him. "I meant that."

When Mason reached the truck, he yanked open the door and threw the hard hat in. "I know you do. And you will pay me back, after you buy me a beer and tell me what bug crawled up your ass."

"You're on."

Twenty minutes later, they were seated in the back of the Wishing Well, where most of the men went after work for a drink on payday.

"So what's got you so pissy?" Mason asked, pouring a glass of beer from the pitcher.

Chase took the glass from Mason and chugged its entire contents in one fell swoop.

"Damn, it's that bad?" Mason asked. "Then it must be a woman, namely London."

Chase placed the empty glass on the table and motioned for Mason to refill it. "Yeah, man. I caught her with another dude."

"What?" Mason looked skeptical. "Naw, I can't believe that. London is on the up and up. A churchgoing sista."

"That's what I thought because that's what she led me

to believe too." Chase rubbed his temples. Just thinking about it gave him a headache. "But I saw it with my very own eyes."

Mason finished pouring Chase another glass, pushed it toward him, and filled his own. "What did you see?"

"I saw her ex at London's restaurant, all up in her grill."

"What were they doing? Were they kissing or in some sort of passionate embrace?"

Chase grimaced. "Does it matter? I know what I saw and they were entirely too close for comfort."

Mason sipped on his beer and then asked, "Could you have mistaken the situation?"

"The man was putting the moves on my woman and she was letting him."

Mason shook his head. "Sounds kind of suspicious to me. I wouldn't write London off until you talk to her. If she lies to your face you'll know, but at least it stops all this wondering."

"I'm not wondering," Chase said and took another gulp of beer. "The woman I love is still hung up on her ex-husband."

Mason plopped his glass back on the table. "What did you just say?"

Chase rolled his eyes. "You heard me. London is still hung up on that joker."

"Naw, that's not what you said. You said *the woman I love.*"

"I suppose I did. But so what?"

"So what?" Mason's voice rose. "You, who vowed to never love another soul, has fallen in love? As bitter as you were over your divorce, this is a miracle, Chase. You have to tell London how you feel."

"So she can stomp all over my heart when she leaves to go back to that pretty boy? No thank you. I'll take these feelings with me to the grave. Feelings that caught me completely unaware."

Mason shook his head. "I think it's a mistake. How do you know London doesn't feel the same way too? You at least have to try. If not, you'll always wonder if you could have stolen her back or at the very least made her see what she was giving up on."

"It's over, Mason," Chase said, "and I just have to accept it. I refuse to make a fool of myself because of another woman. Not this time around. I've been a fool for love for the last and final time."

"That's a shame," Mason said, "because I truly think you could be giving up on someone special."

Chase leaned back in his chair and stared at Mason. Was his best friend in the whole world right? Was he making a mistake by not confronting London with the scene he'd witnessed yesterday? Maybe he owed it to himself and to their relationship, no matter how short-lived, to find out?

After Mason left the bar to get home to Kelly and the boys, Chase had hung around. He shouldn't have. But the thing was he didn't want to go home alone to an empty apartment. He'd thought that by staying out late enough, he'd fall sleep in a heap on the couch the moment he returned home.

He was tossing down several bills on the bar to cover his tab when he heard a familiar voice. A voice that reminded Chase of all he may have lost.

Chase leaned backward and caught sight of Shawn's profile as he sat with another man farther down the bar. Chase rolled his eyes upward. Of all the bars in town, why did Shawn have to show up at his?

He planned to walk right past him but the bastard wouldn't let him.

"Ah, there's the man that stole my woman," Shawn told the man at his side as he sipped his drink.

"Excuse me?"

"You heard me right. I'd trained London. Had her wrapped around"—Shawn held up his pinky—"my little finger and here you come all big and bad and ruin a good thing."

"You'd *trained her*?" Chase's voice held a hint of his rising anger.

Shawn laughed. "You know how you have to do with those big girls"—he bumped shoulders with the other man—"you tell them how beautiful they are and the panties drop with quickness. It musta been the same for you. How else to explain how London is hung up on you?"

Chase didn't even realize he'd lifted his arm until he punched Shawn smack dab in the face and saw him topple off his barstool. Then he lunged for him and the rest of the world faded.

Br-r-ring. Br-r-ring. Br-r-ring. London rolled over and glanced at her clock. It was well after midnight. Who the hell was calling her? She'd just drifted off to sleep after a long day at Shay's and needed rest. Charlotte had called out sick today and London had had to run the entire lunch and dinner service with only one line cook. She'd been exhausted and unprepared for the serious conversation she knew she'd needed to have with Chase, so she'd decided to wait until Saturday, her day off when they'd have no interruptions.

She reached for her cell phone, but didn't recognize the number. "Hello?"

"Is this London Hart?"

"Yes." London instantly awoke at the curt tone in the stranger's voice. "Who is this?"

"It's Larry, the barkeep down at Wishing Well. I believe you know Chase Tanner, right?"

"I do. Has something happened to him?" she asked,

reaching for the bedside lamp and flicking it on, flooding her bedroom with light. "Is he okay?"

"Yeah, he is, but I'm not sure about the fella he clocked," the barkeep returned. "May have a broken nose."

London tossed back the covers and searched the room frantically for something to wear. "What did you say?"

"He laid a guy out for talking about his woman and I understand and all, but with a Slick Rick like this guy, he'll want to press charges, which is why Chase was taken to the sheriff's office."

"Can you describe the man Chase hit?"

Several moments later, London knew exactly who Chase had punched: Shawn. *What's going on?!*

"Alright. Thank you for telling me," London said as she slipped on her favorite track-suit pants. "And Larry, may I ask, did he ask you to call me?"

"Naw, but I've seen you here with him a time or two and with Miss Violet. I called her to get your number. She said you'd want to know."

"Thanks, Larry. I appreciate it." London ended the call.

So Chase hadn't thought of her in his time of need. Instead he was content to sit in a jail cell rather than call her. Her first instinct was to leave him there to teach him a lesson that violence was never a solution, but the other side of her—the side that loved him—couldn't leave him in that cell. So she slipped on the matching jacket to her track pants and headed for the door.

"What the hell were you thinking?" Mason asked Chase as he stood in front of Chase's cell.

Chase had hit Shawn only once. Hell, he would have done a lot more if Larry the barkeep hadn't held him back. The way that bastard had been talking about London had made Chase's blood boil. He couldn't let Shawn get away with disrespecting his woman. From the comments Shawn was making, Chase wasn't altogether sure what exactly had happened between London and her ex-husband at Shay's.

Had he gotten it all wrong? Had London turned Shawn down, which is why he'd badmouthed her at the bar?

"I asked you a damn question," Mason roared.

Chase held his head. He had a splitting headache from drinking all night. It was something he never did, but today–or was it yesterday—he'd felt justified doing it. "Must you talk so loud?"

"Yes," Mason said, holding his tone, "when you do something stupid to land yourself in jail. C'mon, Chase. This isn't you. You've always had a clean record."

"They haven't arrested me," Chase said.

"Only put you in a cell to cool off," Mason responded. "From what I hear you were out of control tonight."

Chase rose to his feet a little too quickly and stumbled. He righted himself and walked toward Mason. He held onto the bars on either side with both hands. "Listen to me, Mace. You didn't hear the way that guy was putting down London."

"You should have walked away," Mason replied. "Why didn't you leave with me anyway? I warned you no good was going to come from you staying and look at what happened."

"I could do without an 'I told you so,'" Chase murmured.

"Someone has to talk to you. You've been hot-headed and out of control the last twenty-four hours. You need to get your shit together."

"Or what?" Chase huffed. "You're not going to bail me out after everything we've been through?"

Mason rolled his eyes. "Of course not. I've never left a man behind before and I don't intend on doing it now, but this has got to stop. You need to talk to London and clear the air between you two."

"I'm right here," a feminine voice said from behind Mason.

Chase's heart jolted at hearing London's voice. He

knew it was her before Mason turned around and brought her into his line of sight. She looked beautiful as always, in a fuchsia track suit and matching pink cross-trainers.

"Mason, do you mind if I talk to Chase alone?" London asked.

He shook his head. "No, he's all yours." Mason gave Chase a wave and left them in the room together.

London stood several feet away from the bars of the cell. Chase took a few steps back from the bars, watching her, waiting. For what, a sign that she still wanted him and hadn't abandoned him for her slimy ex-husband?

When she said nothing and merely glared at him, Chase said, "How did you find out I was here?"

"Larry from the Wishing Well called me."

"I didn't ask him to call you," Chase said.

"I'm very well aware of that, Chase," London responded, walking toward the cell. "What the hell? You'd rather stay in here or call Mason than call me?"

"Don't act all innocent, London," Chase replied. "You're not completely blameless in this."

London frowned. "What are you talking about?"

"I get it, okay," Chase said. "I know I'm damaged goods, a screw-up, and it would be easier to go back to a clean-cut guy like Shawn, but I'm telling you London, you could do a helluva lot better."

"Go back to Shawn? Why would I ever go back to his lying, cheating ass after what he did to me?"

"Because he's everything I'm not, London. He's a white-collar kind of guy who isn't messed up in the head." He motioned to his head, circling his index finger around. "I've got issues, real issues. Lots of them that can't be solved in an hour-long TV show, London."

"I know that."

"And that's why you turned to Shawn," Chase said. "I get it. You want someone without all the baggage, but that doesn't mean I have to like it. Not when I've seen how happy you were with me." He rushed to the bars. "Not when I *saw, felt* you respond to my touch, to my kiss. Dammit." He stepped away and began pacing the floor. "I can't do this." He shook his head. "I can't talk about this." He rushed back over to the bench and lowered his head.

It was all becoming clear now. London put her hands on her ample hips and said, "Wait just a second. You mean to tell me you think I want Shawn back? That we are somehow getting back together? Where in the hell would you get a crazy notion like that?"

"Don't do that, London." Chase's voice was dangerously low. "Don't act like nothing happened between you and Shawn."

London was quickly becoming annoyed. "That's because nothing *did* happen between us. He came over to Shay's two days ago."

"I *know*," Chase said, "because I saw you."

"I don't understand. You saw us? When?"

"That's because you were so engrossed in each other, you didn't see me staring at you through the window."

"Engrossed?" London thought back to her brief time with Shawn and that's when it hit her. Chase must have looked in the window at the exact moment Shawn tried to put the moves on her, but if he'd stayed long enough, he would have seen her push him away.

"Yeah, he was all up on you and you didn't seem to mind one bit. It's no wonder I wanted to knock the guy's lights out. You were *my* woman." He pounded his chest. "Instead I see another man with his hands on you."

London's heart turned over in her chest at his use of the past tense. "Were? I *was* your woman and now I'm not? Are you deliberately trying to hurt me, Chase? My God, it's only been a few days and you've moved on already?"

She turned away, unable to face him as tears began streaming down her cheeks. How could he be willing to walk away from all they'd shared after seeing that encounter?

Without giving her the chance to explain? *Because he doesn't trust you,* an inner voice said. *He never has.*

"*I've* moved on?" Chase asked. "I didn't move on. You did."

London suddenly spun back around to face him. "Liar. You've just been waiting for the moment when I'd betray you because you've never truly trusted me. Because you trust no one. Why, Chase?" She struck the bar of the jail cell with her fists. "Because Bianca betrayed you with your best friend? Well I didn't betray you. I would never do that to you. I, more than anyone else, know what it's like to be in your shoes and would never do that to another human being, least of all you, the man I love. But you don't trust me and you don't believe in us. How could you, if you're so willing to turn your back on me at the first sign of conflict?"

After her impassioned speech, Chase stared back at her in stunned silence.

Then London realized what she'd said. She'd told him she loved him. She clutched her hand to her mouth. She hadn't meant to say that.

Not out loud.

Not like this.

Not when he was behind bars.

But now it was out there in the open. He now knew how she felt and it would be up to him on how he responded from this point forward. And so she said quietly, "You can't go on like this, Chase. Never trusting anyone, never letting anyone in. Because I promise you, it'll be a very lonely existence. I'm asking you to get help. If you can't do it for yourself, do it for me, because I love you and I don't want to see you like this."

Chase stared back at her. "Can you repeat that?"

"Which part?"

"You know the part."

London sighed. He was forcing her to put it all out

there without any thought to whether her feelings would be reciprocated. *But isn't that what love is all about? About taking risks?*

She took a deep, encouraging breath and looked into his dark-brown eyes. "I said I love you. And I'm here to support you if you'll let me," she said softly. "But you have to let me in, Chase. And you have to get help and go to therapy."

"Come here." Chase motioned her forward.

At first London didn't move, but the pleading look in his eyes forced her to walk toward him. When she was close enough, he reached out to grasp her hands. "I'm sorry. I'm sorry for doubting you, for doubting us."

London nodded and looked downward.

"And London?"

She glanced up through wet lashes. "I love you too. And when I get out of here, I promise you I'll get help. I'll go back to therapy if you promise to be by my side."

London's face brightened at hearing the three words she was dying to hear back. "You mean it?"

"Oh yes," Chase said, grinning. "And when I get out of here, I'll show you how much."

"Ahem, ahem," a loud cough sounded behind them and they pulled apart.

It was Mason and the sheriff. "Well your lucky day is today," Mason said, "because you're getting out now."

"I'm an ex-veteran myself," the sheriff said, pulling his keys off his belt, "so I understand having a short fuse after getting out. So I'm going to let you out on your own recognizance, but I can't guarantee Mr. Garrett won't file charges tomorrow."

Chase nodded. "I understand."

Once the sheriff found the key for Chase's cell, he unlocked it and Chase immediately rushed into London's arms. And without waiting to get outside, and in front of Mason and the sheriff, he kissed London long, hard, and deep. He placed one hand behind her head and angled her for the best fit of his mouth over hers.

The kiss was amazing, all the more so because they loved each other. His kiss sent sparks of familiar need coursing through London's nerve endings, especially when his tongue slid between the seams of her mouth to mate with hers. It was wicked, decadent, and delicious. She wanted much more than a kiss. She wanted Chase inside her.

Mason coughed again. "Well, I think my work here is done. I'll see you two lovebirds later."

But Chase and London didn't bother to look up. They were too engrossed in each other to notice him or the sheriff leave. Chase pressed his mouth to London's and she knew exactly what to do. She softened her lips and molded them to his.

When they finally parted, Chase breathed soft puffs of air against her lips. "You know we should get out of here. I think we already gave Mason and the sheriff a show."

London smiled softly. "I'd like that a lot."

Chapter 19

THEY WALKED HAND IN HAND together to London's Jeep parked on the street. On the way to her house, Chase apologized. "I'm truly sorry, London, for believing the worst. I knew better because it warred with what my heart told me about you and like a fool I let my insecurities get in the way of what we have." He glanced over at her. "I won't do that again."

"You'd better not," London warned.

Instead of going to London's, she drove to his place. He stared at her, bewildered. "We're always at my place," she said. "How about we christen your apartment so you have memories of us making love in every room..." Her voice trailed off.

"In every position?" he asked hopefully.

London grinned. "What do you think?"

As soon as they were inside, they spent the next few minutes undressing each other as they made their way to Chase's bedroom. She gave a whoop when Chase was down to his boxers. How she'd missed this man!

Chase picked her up with one arm and kissed her. His mouth devoured hers, holding her head and keeping her lips exactly where he wanted them while his warm masculine fingers caressed and kneaded her every curve. She kissed him back with all the pent-up emotion she'd felt curled up inside for the last four days.

Her breasts were already hard peaks, throbbing for his touch, for his mouth. Heat washed over her as need grew in her core. Her body was more sensitive with Chase than she'd ever known possible. He had a way of eliciting moans and shivers from her that no other man had.

She was greedy for more and refused to allow Chase to have all the fun. She sensually explored his body. When she found the column of hard flesh, she began working her way up and down it with her hands.

"Don't stop," he instructed as she continued her ministrations. He closed his eyes as London moved from root to tip and back up again. "Ah, that's it, baby, yes. Just like that."

Instead of using her hands to finish him off, London quickly replaced her hands with her mouth. Chase let out a long shuddering breath as she teased him with light, gentle, and hard flicks of her tongue and teeth.

"Christ, what are you doing to me, woman?"

She smiled up at him, "Making you remember that you're the only man for me."

Desire coursed through Chase's veins at London's bold words. His swollen sex jutted out from him and she greedily took all of him into her mouth. It was a major turn-on.

He'd barely been able to refrain himself in that jail cell. When London had told him she *loved* him, everything else had faded away for Chase. He could finally see things clearer than he had in days. London would never betray him as Bianca had done. She wasn't that type of woman. Deep down he'd always known but he'd been afraid to believe it, afraid to take a risk and allow himself to believe it.

But he did now.

Saying the words aloud and telling London he loved her too was cathartic. It was like it released the chains around his heart and his soul and he was finally unfettered and free to be with her. Sure, he still had a long way to go and would need counseling, but with London at his side, all things were possible.

And tonight, he would make everything right between them. He would show her just how much he loved and *wanted her.* He pulled London away from his throbbing penis and pressed her flush against his body on the bed. Even though she was shorter than him by a few inches and had more curves, she fit him perfectly. He kissed her again, demanding a response, and she gave it freely, matching his own, parting her lips in open surrender.

She tasted so sweet and so good, Chase knew he'd never want to live another day without her kiss. He laid her back on the bed and kissed her entire body, intent on building the intensity of pleasure for her, but the more he teased London, the closer to the edge Chase got.

And when he pressed her legs apart and put his mouth on her intimately, London cried and whimpered. Her unique musky scent smelled like heaven to Chase and he pushed his tongue inside her.

"Sweet Jesus!" London screamed when he pulled it out again and then back in again. He loved her responsiveness, especially her mewls when he flicked her clitoris with his tongue and circled it with the tip. He slid a finger into her wet passage and reveled in its slickness.

London began to move against his fingers and tongue. She was desperate for more and so was he. He greedily tasted her over and over. London had a way of making him feel like he couldn't hold back. Her cries and whimpers spoke to him and he was ready to answer.

Turning her to her side, he angled his body from behind and pressed forward into her. The position gave him the liberties he wanted, which was to mold her breasts with his hands and reach down to her clitoris and finger her.

She gasped as he began moving faster and faster.

London gave everything she could to this man, *her man.* And there was no more wondering "what if" because she now knew Chase loved her as much as she loved him. She moved her pelvis to his rhythm, giving herself to the moment. They both came together, their shouts echoing in the darkness as sheer bliss coursed through them.

"You're back," Dr. Burke commented when Chase stood outside his office with his hands in his jeans pocket later that afternoon. "Didn't think I'd ever see you again."

Chase snorted. "Neither did I. Can I come in?"

Dr. Burke opened the door. "Of course. I have an open-door policy."

"Even for me?" Chase cocked his head in inquiry.

"Especially for you, Chase," Dr. Burke responded. "I was never upset with you. I know what you've endured and how hard it is for a man as proud as you to admit when he needs help."

"I deserve that," Chase said, sitting down on the sofa opposite Dr. Burke's favorite armchair.

"I'm not saying it to be mean or spiteful. I'm just speaking the truth. You have an awfully big chip on your shoulder, so I know it must have taken something or someone extraordinary to bring you back here."

Chase nodded. "It was."

"Care to tell me about it?"

This was the part Chase hated, having to open up about what was going on in his head, in his heart, but he'd made a promise to himself and London that he would get the help he needed. And he was nothing if not a man of his word.

"The nightmares have returned. London and I nearly broke up because I thought she was cheating on me with her ex and I promptly smashed his face in the next time I saw him and ended up in jail."

"Wow! Okay." The doctor then became silent as he processed all the information Chase had just shared.

"On the positive side," Chase began.

"There is one?"

Chase chuckled. "Actually there is. One, I was wrong about London. She was most certainly *not* having an affair with that scumbag because she *loves* me."

"Ah." The doctor smiled. "Now that's something positive to hear. So how do you feel about London? Because you've always been reluctant to share your feelings."

He was right. Chase had been hesitant, but not anymore. "I love her, Doc. I think I have for a while. And when I thought I might lose her, when I thought she might have chosen another man over me, I was wrecked and self-destructive."

"What did you do?"

"I argued with my boss at work and picked a fight. Then he promptly sent my ass home."

"And?"

"So I got drunk with my best friend, but then he left the bar and I stayed. Long enough to hear London's ex talk trash about her. I was so furious with what I *thought* happened, I clocked him real good."

"Did it make you feel any better?"

"Actually, it did," Chase responded with a laugh, "but only for a second. It was a stupid thing to do. And if Shawn wants to be an ass, he could press charges."

"So you realize that violence is never the answer?"

Chase snorted. "Sometimes it's necessary. I have to believe that or I wouldn't have been able to serve my country, but...," he paused, "in this instance I should have walked away."

"Sounds like you learned something from this."

"I hope I don't have to learn it the hard way in jail, but whatever it is, I'll face the consequences of my actions and that will be a whole lot easier with London by my side. Knowing she loves and supports me makes a world of difference."

"Is she the only reason you're here?" Dr. Burke asked,

"'cause if so, it's not enough, Chase. You have to want this for yourself in order for therapy to work."

"I know that, Doc. And although I'm not a big fan of head-shrinking, it's the closest I've come to peace in a long time, so I'm gonna continue with it."

"Even if the questions get hard?"

"Yes."

"Even if you have to relive some painful memories you'd rather keep locked inside?"

"Even then, Doc."

A smile spread across Dr. Burke's thin lips. "Then I'm happy, Chase, because we've made a breakthrough. Let's get started."

London was not looking forward to what she had to do. She'd been sitting in her Jeep for the last ten minutes debating the rightness of her actions, but she didn't have a choice. She had to talk to Shawn and convince him not to press charges against Chase. She knew it was a shot in the dark, but she had to try for Chase's sake... hell, for both of theirs.

She didn't want her man to have a record or face jail time. She was just going to have to suck up her pride and talk to her ex-husband.

When she'd called him earlier, he'd been surprised to hear from her, but had agreed to meet with her in the lobby of the building where he worked. It was a public, well-lit place and London knew Shawn would be on his best behavior because he might see some of his coworkers.

Reluctantly, she opened the driver's side door and disembarked from her vehicle. She strode with a purpose through the glass doors of the office building and found Shawn waiting for her in one of the sitting areas in the lobby.

Shawn didn't stand when she approached like Chase

did, but that didn't surprise her. He never had stood on ceremony or was in any way chivalrous toward her when they'd been together.

"Shawn." She nodded as she sat down in the lounge chair opposite him.

"Coffee?" he inquired.

"No, I'm fine. Thanks," London said, smoothing down her skirt. She watched Shawn's eyes follow her actions and she could see the wheels in his mind turn and knew he was curious as to what she was wearing underneath. Pig.

She just had to get through this meeting with a modicum of decorum. "I'm sure you know why I asked for this meeting."

"Because your barbarian of a boyfriend attacked me," Shawn replied.

"He's not a barbarian, Shawn. But he is a bit hot-headed."

"Is that what you call it? Does he always attack people unprovoked?"

London raised a brow. "C'mon, Shawn. Don't act like you didn't light the match. I'm sure you said something less than flattering about me."

"And that gave him cause to strike me?" Shawn asked, his voice rising as he leaned forward. "I don't think so. But he'll think twice next time around after I prosecute him."

"Is that really necessary, Shawn? Chase is sorry for his behavior."

"I don't see him apologizing."

"Because I thought it best I come," London responded.

"Because of our shared history?" he queried, leaning back and throwing his arm over the back of the sofa. "And what do you think that'll get you?"

"I beg your pardon?"

"What exactly are you prepared to offer me to ensure I won't press charges against your caveman?"

London rolled her eyes and counted from one to ten, reminding herself that violence was never an option.

However, she could see why Chase would want to slug Shawn. He was an asshole.

"Listen up, Shawn. I know this may come as a shock to you, but some of us have principles, morals, and values. I'm not prepared to offer you a damn thing. I came here because yes, we have a shared history, we were married for *five years* and silly me I thought there might be a place in the stone-cold place you call a heart that remembered that, remembered what we used to be to each other and would care enough about me to grant me this one thing and let this issue go." She rose to her feet. "But I was wrong. Clearly, our marriage—hell, our entire relationship— meant nothing to you. Good day."

She turned to leave, but Shawn stood up.

"Wait!"

"What?" London turned to glare at him. "Have a few more jabs to get in at me about my weight or perhaps at the man I love, whom you've labeled a barbarian. A man that actually loves me and accepts me as I am."

Shawn stared back at her. "You love him?"

"Of course I do, Shawn. Why else would I belittle myself and come here today to plead on his behalf?"

Shawn looked bewildered. "I guess I just never considered you were that serious about him."

"I love him. And he loves me too."

"I can see that."

London stared at Shawn and waited, but still he said nothing. "Alright, well I'm going."

"London, wait!" Shawn caught up with her at the revolving door at the building's entrance.

"Haven't we said all there is to say?"

"Probably," Shawn replied, "except this: I won't press charges."

London's eyes widened in disbelief. "You won't?"

Shawn nodded. "If he really means that much to you,

London, then I won't, but you tell that knucklehead two things."

"And what's that?"

"If he comes near me again I won't be so generous."

"And the second?"

"That he's lucky to have found a beautiful, caring woman like you. Not everyone would have the balls to come and face me. You've got guts, London, but then you always did and just never saw it."

"No, I'm the lucky one, Shawn, because I found a man as good and decent as Chase, but I'll pass along the message."

Shawn nodded and turned to leave.

"And Shawn?"

"Yeah?" He pivoted on his heel to look at her.

"Thank you." London pushed the revolving door and walked through it to the next phase of her life.

"You're kidding?" Chase said as they sat back on London's sofa with a bottle of celebratory champagne later that evening.

"Nope." London shook her head. "Shawn agreed to not press charges, so you won't have a record."

"Hallelujah! You did it!" Chase grasped London in his arms and kissed her fiercely. "I can't believe it, but you did it. I'm so thankful, babe."

"How thankful?" London inquired with a wicked grin.

"How about I show you?"

"Bring it on."

Chase and London's coupling later that night was driven by a mad, passionate need for each other. Chase drove London to new heights. And not wanting to be outdone, she matched him kiss for kiss, touch for touch, lick for lick, until she had him climbing the walls and groaning her name. Their bodies were so in tune with each other that when they finally climaxed it was like they were two halves of the same whole.

In the afterglow, Chase kissed her sweaty brow. "London?"

"Hmmm." She glanced up at him through sleepy eyes.

"You're the one," Chase said.

"I know."

"Someone's feeling mighty confident."

"After what we just endured, shared, hell yes." She smiled.

He caressed her cheek with one of his hands. "I guess I never realized it until now, but I don't think I ever really knew what love was until I met you."

"Honey." She stroked his cheek, touched by his words.

"What I'm saying very badly is, I've only truly ever loved one woman and that's you, London. And I don't ever want to lose you."

"And now you won't have to because I'm not going anywhere." She snuggled up in his arms and that's where she stayed until the sun rose over the horizon.

Epilogue

"**M**ARRIED, WHAT DO YOU MEAN you're married?" Bree asked over the telephone when London and Chase called her six months later. She, Jada, and their father Duke were congregated around a telephone in his home office in Dallas.

"We just decided to go down to St. Lucia and get married, just the two of us on the beach," London replied. "We both had large weddings the first time around and this time we wanted it to be just the two of us. Ain't that right, baby?"

London glanced at Chase and he nodded from his side of the loveseat in what was once solely London's home, but was now the home they shared.

"I'm sorry if you feel slighted, Mr. Hart," Chase spoke up so that his voice could be caught by their cell's speakerphone, "but you know I love your daughter."

"Of course I know that, son. You asked me for her hand in marriage," Duke replied. "But I'd have thought that would come along with walking her down the aisle."

"Of course," Chase said, "but as London said, we were down there on vacation and I don't know, it just felt right."

"Well, I for one am tickled pink for you both," Jada chimed in. "Welcome to the family, Chase."

"Thank you, Jada."

"Daddy? Bree?" London inquired. She knew neither of

them were happy with her and Chase's decision to elope, but they'd done what was right for them. "Please tell me we have your support."

"You'll always have that, sweetheart," Duke Hart replied.

"Same here," Bree added, "but what about a reception? Can we at least throw you a celebratory party?"

"Absolutely," London said, "but you'll have to get in line. Grandpa and Grandma have an ever-growing guest list. I think everyone in the community has been invited."

Despite their estrangement, even London's mother had been happy to hear of their nuptials and she planned to attend the reception too.

"Count the entire Hart clan in as well," Duke said, "and let your grandfather know that, as your father, I've got this."

London smiled as she looked at Chase, the love of her life. "Thank you, Daddy. That's very generous of you."

"I'm happy to do it," Duke said. "Now that I've got one down, there's two daughters to go."

"Daddy!" Bree and Jada shouted in unison.

"Talk to you later." London and Chase quickly ended the call. They were eager to get back to their newest agenda: baby-making.

"I think that went rather smoothly, don't you think?" London asked.

"It did," Chase replied, "but even if it didn't, I couldn't be happier with having you as my wife, Mrs. Tanner." He pressed his lips to hers. Although the kiss was warm and sweet, it still had the power to send spirals of ecstasy coursing through her.

"And I couldn't be happier to have you as my husband," London whispered softly.

Lifting London in his arms, Chase carried her toward their bedroom. "Then let's go make a baby."

About the Author

YAHRAH ST. JOHN BECAME A writer at the age of twelve when she wrote her first novella after secretly reading a Harlequin romance. She's the proud author of forty-three books with Kimani Romance and Harlequin Desire plus her own indie books.

When she's not at home crafting one of her steamy romances with compelling heroes and feisty heroines with a dash of family drama, she is gourmet cooking or traveling the globe seeking out her next adventure. For more info:

www.yahrahstjohn.com

Other Books by Yahrah St. John

One Magic Moment
Dare to Love
Never Say Never
Risky Business of Love
Playing for Keeps – Orphan Series
This Time for Real – Orphan Series
If You So Desire– Orphan Series
Two to Tango– Orphan Series
Need You Now – Adams Cosmetic Series
Lost Without You– Adams Cosmetic Series
Formula for Passion– Adams Cosmetic Series
Dirty Laundry
Delicious Destiny – Drayson Series
A Chance With You
Entangled Hearts
Entangled Hearts 2
Untamed Hearts
Restless Hearts
Heat Wave of Desire– Millionaire Mogul Series
Can't Get Enough
Cappuccino Kisses – Drayson Series
Taming Her Tycoon – Knights of LA Series
Chasing Hearts
Miami After Hours – Millionaire Mogul Series
Secrets of the A-List
Taming Her Billionaire – Knights of LA Series
Unchained Hearts
His San Diego Sweetheart – Millionaire Mogul Series

Captivated Hearts
At the Ceo's Pleasure – The Stewart Heirs
His Marriage Demand – The Stewart Heirs
Red Carpet Redemption – The Stewart Heirs
Secrets of a Fake Fiancée – The Stewart Heirs
Insatiable Hunger – Dynasty Seven Sins
Claimed by the Hero – The Mitchell Brothers
Two Hot Kisses – New Year Bae Solutions
Consequences of Passion – The Lockett's of Tuxedo Park
Winning Back His Wife – The Lockett's of Tuxedo Park
Blind Date with the Spare Heir – The
Lockett's of Tuxedo Park
Seducing the Seal – The Mitchell Brothers
Holiday Playbook – The Lockett's of Tuxedo Park
A Game Between Friends – The Lockett's of Tuxedo Park
Vacation Crush – Texas Cattleman's Ranchers & Rivals

Coming Soon
Guarding His Princess – The Mitchell Brothers
Her Best Friend's Brother - Six Gems

Made in the USA
Columbia, SC
19 September 2022

67544187R00130